"We were c **?"**

"Best friends,"

They had been best friends, until she'd married Billy. Her husband had been too threatened by her friendship with his cousin to allow the relationship to continue.

Ava looked away from him, suddenly afraid of the intense look in his eyes and the way it made her feel. "There were times you seemed almost mad at me," she said. "Were you?"

"I could never be mad at you, Ava." He reached out and caressed her cheek. "I was mad at myself, for not speaking up before I left."

"Speaking up about what?" she asked. Her throat felt dry. She could barely push the words out of her mouth.

He smiled at her, a tender smile that went straight to her heart. "It's all water under the bridge." He reached for her hand, giving it a little squeeze before letting it go.

Something flickered in his eyes. She couldn't be sure, but it looked a little like regret.

Books by Belle Calhoune

Love Inspired

Reunited with the Sheriff
Forever Her Hero

BELLE CALHOUNE

was born and raised in Massachusetts. Some of her fondest childhood memories revolve around her four siblings and spending summers in Cape Cod. Although both her parents were in the medical field, she became an avid reader of romance novels as a teen and began dreaming of a career as an author. Shortly thereafter, she began writing her own stories. Married to her college sweetheart, she is raising two lovely daughters in Connecticut. A dog lover, she has a beautiful chocolate lab and an adorable mini poodle. After studying French for ten years and traveling extensively throughout France, she considers herself a Francophile. When she's not writing, she enjoys spending time in Cape Cod and planning her next Parisian escape. She finds writing inspirational romance to be a joyful experience that nurtures her soul. You can write to her at scalhoune@gmail.com or contact her through her website, www.bellecalhoune.com.

Forever Her Hero

Belle Calhoune

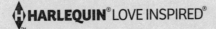

Recycling programs for this product may not exist in your area.

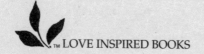

LOVE INSPIRED BOOKS

ISBN-13: 978-0-373-87888-8

FOREVER HER HERO

www.Harlequin.com

Printed in U.S.A.

Weeping may remain for a night,
but rejoicing comes in the morning.
—*Psalms* 30:5

For my daughter, Amber,
who always makes me proud to be her mother.

Acknowledgments

A big thank you to my wonderful editor,
Emily Rodmell—for believing in me and this book.

Many thanks to all the fantastic readers
who have reached out to me with kind words
and encouragement. You lift me up!

Chapter One

Sawyer Trask had been back in Buzzards Bay for two days now. Although he'd stopped on occasion to grab a bite to eat and check in with his team, he'd been in sleep mode ever since he settled in to his new home. He'd slept for a solid fourteen hours straight, which was a record for him. Everything had caught up with him at once—jet lag, being overseas for an extended period of time and his illness. When he finally awakened he'd stepped out onto his parapet just in time to spot Ava Trask walking the path from the beach up to her cottage.

From the first moment he laid eyes on her, something inside him had cracked wide open. He hadn't expected such an overwhelming feeling, but there it was, settled firmly around his heart. It had been a year since he'd seen her. Three hundred and forty-four days since he'd heard her sweet voice.

Sawyer didn't stop to analyze the emotions coursing through him—guilt, attraction, regret? An inner voice had urged him to walk over to the cottage and announce his return, because he knew that the longer he waited, the more difficult it would be to confront the situation head-on. Knowing Ava as well as he did, he could only imagine her stunned reaction.

She was way more beautiful than he remembered, a million times more exotic and appealing. Miles and miles away from the scrawny, plucky tomboy who'd quickly befriended the new kid in town. From the moment she'd reached out to him in the sweetest act of friendship he'd ever known, they'd been as thick as thieves. Ava and Sawyer. In Buzzards Bay their names had been blurred together as if they were one. Partners in crime. Swashbucklers. Pirates. She was so familiar to him, yet everything about her now seemed so foreign. He'd caught a glimpse of her as she took her morning jog across the beach, stood transfixed as she frolicked with the family dog and marveled at the way she played with the twins. His cousin Billy's children. Casey and Dahlia. Dolly, for short. They were six years old, on the cusp of turning seven. Their birthday was coming up in two months. It would be their second one without their father, with dozens of birthdays stretched out before them. A lifetime of events, he thought grimly. Years of special occasions without the man who'd given them life by their side, cheering them on and providing them with guidance.

There was something about the three of them playing on the beach with their dog that pulled at him. They looked like the picture-perfect family, he thought. Minus one. A stab of guilt pierced his heart as his eyes roamed over the family. He wanted to reach out and touch them, to nurture them in any way he could. After all, they were the reason he'd come back. What he really wanted was to be able to give them back every ounce of what had been taken from them. But he couldn't. Some things couldn't be fixed.

Returning home wasn't going to be a cakewalk. He was coming back to the grim reality of what had happened two years ago. It meant acknowledging the way he'd run away like a coward rather than confront his own feelings. He'd have to deal with the lingering grief blanketing his loved ones. And the shadow of guilt that still hung over him. But he was stronger now and more determined than ever. He'd come back to Buzzards Bay with a purpose, one that required commitment and follow-through. It was time to uphold his sacred promise to his cousin. Not another day would go by without him being present in Dolly's and Casey's lives. And somehow he needed to tell Ava about his role in her husband's death. He just hoped it wouldn't mean she'd want nothing more to do with him ever again.

"Tully!" Ava ran down the beach at breakneck speed, her steps slowed down by the gravitational pull of the sand. The sand didn't seem to be slowing down her chocolate Lab puppy as he bounded toward the water. Just as Tully placed his paws in the ocean, she reached down and scooped him up into her arms, nestling him against her chest the same way she'd cradled her babies.

Ava took a deep breath, her nostrils filling with sea air as she struggled to catch her breath. Whew! When had she gotten so out of shape? She used to be able to run the length of this beach without breaking a sweat. She smiled at the memory of Billy pulling her in his arms after she walked into the kitchen after a five-mile run, her body covered with a light mist of sweat. When she'd pulled away from him and told him she needed a shower, he'd drawn her back, bathing her in kisses as he waltzed with her in the kitchen. *He loved me,* she thought, *warts and all.* And she'd loved him the same way, even when it seemed almost impossible to keep loving that man.

The twins came running after her, their tiny feet nearly swallowed up by the sand. "You caught him, Mama," Casey shouted. "You sure moved fast."

"I had to move quickly." Ava nuzzled Tully's face, earning herself slobbery kisses in return.

"Mama, I saw a man over there." Dolly pointed a chubby finger toward the horizon, and for a moment it seemed to Ava as if her daughter was pointing toward the sky.

"Where, baby?" she asked, craning her neck upward.

"At the lighthouse."

"Nuh-uh. No one lives there," said Casey with an emphatic nod of his head.

"Does so. I saw him." Dolly leaned in toward Casey, her hands perched on her hips.

"Does not, tattle baby." Casey leaned in, as well, so that they were standing nose-to-nose.

"Does so, stinky pants."

"Stop! Stop!" Ava held up her hands to ward off the war of words between the twins. With her kids it only took seconds for things to spiral out of control. Next thing you knew they'd be rolling around in the sand like miniwrestlers. "Twin rule number one. Be respectful of each other. Everyone has their right to an opinion."

"I did so see a man there. He was walking around at the tippy top of the lighthouse when Auntie took us for a walk yesterday." Dolly's arms were folded across her chest, and she was glaring at her brother.

"Nope. I didn't see a man up there." Casey thrust out his lower lip, his voice sounding emphatic. "The only time I seen a man up there was when Mr. P lived there." A sad look shadowed Casey's face. "And Mr. P died just like Daddy. We're not gonna see neither of them ever, ever, ever again."

A solemn look passed over Dolly's face. "But we can see them in our dreams, Casey. And one day we'll see them in Heaven."

"Heaven must be awesome," Casey said with a sigh. "I wanna go there."

Ava bent down till she was level with her son, then tweaked him playfully on the nose. With his walnut-colored skin, expressive eyes and adorable dimples, his resemblance to his father never failed to amaze her. Dolly, on the other hand, looked like a mini version of her, down to her hazel eyes and the cleft in her chin.

"You won't be going to visit until you're a very old man. You've got lots to do before you see Heaven."

Dolly's chin sank down onto her chest, and she began to sniffle. "Daddy had lots to do, but God still took him."

"I know, baby. It doesn't seem fair, does it? The only

thing I can figure is that God needed him up there by His side."

She patted Dolly on the back and began a slow, rhythmic rubbing between her shoulder blades. It was a technique she'd used on her daughter ever since she was a baby in the cradle. Dolly was the sensitive, caring twin, while Casey was the more rambunctious, playful one. Regardless, they both missed their father and were still seeking an answer as to why he'd been taken from them. And they weren't the only ones, she reminded herself. Two years after her husband's death she was still struggling with the tragic event that had taken Billy's life. She still asked herself over and over again if she could have done anything to prevent it.

Tears misted Ava's eyes as she fought back another wave of sadness. When did it end? When did the mourning fade away? When would she be strong enough to let this grief pass over her? Everyone told her it was a process, one she'd walk through in her own time. But she still missed him, still grieved the love they'd shared. Perhaps she would always feel this way, she realized, as if a piece of her had been taken along with her Billy.

She knew some of it was guilt. If she'd gotten him the help he so desperately needed for his drinking, would he have been out on the water that day? Would things have spiraled so badly out of control if Billy hadn't been under the influence?

Lord, please give me the courage to move past Billy's death. Give me the grace to think about our life together without bitterness or regret. Allow me to focus on the good things and not dwell on the bad. Help me raise my two children to be strong and resilient. Please, Lord, help me heal.

She looked up at the lighthouse just in time to see a figure standing on the parapet, then quickly dart out of view. Dolly was right! Someone was there in the lighthouse, and from the looks of it, he'd been watching them.

Sawyer sprinted down the steps and dashed out the front door into the crisp Cape Cod sunshine, his movements agile and quick. He'd watched from the window as the chocolate Lab got away from Ava for a second time. From the looks of it, she'd been too preoccupied with the kids to notice the Lab's escape until it was too late.

As soon as he reached the beach, the sand became a challenge. He felt as if he were running in quicksand. He'd sprinted along this beach hundreds of times. As a kid he was the one all the others had tried to beat as they raced from the lighthouse to the rocks. More times than not he'd been the winner.

He zigzagged across the sand, following the trail blazed by the chocolate Lab. Using every ounce of energy he possessed, he gave it a final push. He reached down and scooped up the furry blob just as he reached the water's edge, cradling the puppy in his arms like a football. Bending over at the waist, he took a moment to catch his breath. When he finally turned around, Ava was a few feet away from him, appearing winded and slightly annoyed.

She stopped in her tracks abruptly, her mouth hanging open in shock at the sight of him. She was achingly beautiful. With her café au lait skin, brilliant hazel eyes and chocolate-brown hair, she could easily have graced the covers of magazines. Her athletic build spoke of her love of running and healthy lifestyle. In all the time he'd known her, he'd been able to gauge her feelings with just one look.

At the moment her eyes were stormy with emotion. Surprise. Anger. Confusion.

"Sawyer? What are you doing here?" she asked.

He walked toward her, easily closing the gap between them. The puppy was still snuggled in his arms, worn-out from his mad dash across the beach. He was making little panting noises, his body heaving with the effort.

"The mission ended. I'm back in town for good, Ava." He mindlessly patted the puppy, trying to soothe his soft whimpers. He watched her carefully, anxious to see her reaction to his news. She tensed up. Her mouth was set in a firm line while her eyes glittered dangerously. Sawyer knew her well enough to know the warning signs. If he had any sense he would run for cover. Without a word, Ava reached out and snatched the puppy from his arms.

"Welcome back, Sawyer," she spit out. "If I'd known you were coming I would have thrown you a party. Forgive me for not rolling out the red carpet."

He let out a pent-up sigh. "I know you're upset with me, but I'd like to see the kids, to help you any way I can."

"Help me?" She bristled. "The same way you helped me after Billy died? 'Cause from what I remember you were a rock for the first year, until you took off for parts unknown and stayed gone this whole time."

He gritted his teeth, uncomfortable with her angry stance. "The coast guard sent me to Africa on a global partnership mission. I couldn't tell you where I was going before I left, Ava. Those missions are classified."

She juggled the puppy in her arms as she attached the leash to his collar. "It's been a year since you left. One whole year. The twins have asked about you nonstop, and I kept telling them you'd be back, that their uncle wouldn't stay away for long. And guess what?" she exploded. "They finally stopped asking about you, because as faithful and trusting as kids are, even they can't continue to believe in something that doesn't exist!"

He hung his head, not wanting to see the hurt in Ava's eyes. He could hear it ringing out in her voice. Seeing it would bring him to his knees. The thought of causing Ava and the twins pain was agonizing. When he'd left Cape Cod it had been an act of self-preservation, an attempt to extinguish all the guilt he'd felt over his cousin's death and to get his life back on track. In the end, running away had only made things worse, since thoughts of Ava and the kids had relentlessly followed him.

"I know I shouldn't have taken the assignment. I should have stayed right here where I belong. Believe me, if I could go back and change things, I would." It was the closest he'd come to apologizing to her. He should have told her sooner, perhaps written her a heartfelt letter. There was so much more lying under the surface, things that both of them had always chosen to ignore. They were part of the reason he'd left and why he'd chosen to stay out of contact with her, even though he'd sent half a dozen postcards and packages to the kids. But it was far too soon for him to start digging up the past. For now, all he wanted to do was extend an olive branch.

"Well, Billy always said your job was the most important thing to you," she said crisply. "I guess you proved him right."

Ava turned her back on him and began walking down the beach toward her house. He could see Casey and Dolly in the distance, darting among the waves crashing toward the shore. More than anything he wanted to see them, to spin them around in his arms and tell them how much he'd missed them. But he couldn't. He didn't know if he had the right to just walk back into their lives, especially since their mother wasn't rolling out the welcome mat.

For all he knew the twins no longer remembered him. In a child's life, a year was a lifetime. He didn't want to believe they could so easily forget all the campouts on the beach, the sailing lessons or the trips to the aquarium at Woods Hole. Since the day they were born he'd loved them more than he could put into words. It would be painful to see a blank look on their faces. Even if their memories of him had faded, he still intended to be a permanent fixture in their lives from this point forward. He wasn't going anywhere, not ever again.

Lord, please let me help Ava and the kids any way I can. Let me make up for any pain I've caused them and help them continue to heal. And please give me the strength to stay on course and not run away from over-whelming feelings. Lord, give me strength.

As he watched Ava take the twins by the hand and lead them across the beach to the stone path leading to their house, he felt a huge sense of loss wash over him. How many times had he sat on this beach with Billy and watched the kids make sand castles? How many times had he walked the stone path with Ava? There was so much he had to say to her in order to make things right between them.

There's no time like the present, a little voice buzzed in his ear. Why shouldn't he follow them up to the house? Even though Ava was still bitter about his having left Cape Cod, he needed to get a few things straight with her. He needed to make her understand that accepting the assignment in Africa didn't mean he'd abandoned them. And before she found out from someone else, he needed to tell her that he was the proud owner of a lighthouse and her new next-door neighbor.

Ava opened the back door of her house with trembling fingers. She was breathing hard, her chest rising and falling in an uneven rhythm as chaotic thoughts swirled in her head. Her palms were damp. She reminded herself to breathe in and out, slowly and evenly. As she ushered the kids through the door, she barely noticed their sandy feet and the dirty beach toys they'd brought inside. Feeling a bit dazed, she deposited Tully on the floor and began filling up his water bowl. She was just going through the motions. Her thoughts were all jumbled and unfocused. All she could think about was what had just happened on the beach. All she could focus on was Sawyer.

Seeing him standing there on the beach holding her puppy in his arms had been a shock. It had felt like a jolt to the system. He was still so ruggedly handsome with a leanly muscled build, broad shoulders, chocolate-brown eyes and warm, caramel-colored skin. His features were no less arresting than they'd always been—sharp, high cheekbones and wide, almond-shaped eyes.

She'd already replayed their encounter several times in her mind. And despite the anger that continued to course through her, she felt guilty about the way she'd treated him. It wasn't like her to be snotty and rude. It wasn't like her to turn her back on someone and walk away. But she'd been holding on to this anger for so long it was now bubbling over, unable to be contained.

Sawyer was back in Buzzards Bay! He was home! A little burst of happiness flowed through her as the knowledge settled in around her heart that he was finally back home. That first moment of recognition when she'd locked gazes with him had been full of mixed emotions. Her initial reaction upon realizing it was him had been joy. Her second emotion had been pure, unbridled rage. How dare he just show up on the beach without a care in the world after a whole year of being gone? Didn't he know what his absence had done to her family? Hadn't he realized how deeply they'd missed him? How she had been lost without her best friend?

The intensity of her feelings frightened her. She was always so reserved and contained with her emotions. It was rare that she showed her innermost feelings. But leave it to Sawyer to drag it to the surface. Ever since they were kids he'd possessed a knack for bringing out her intense side. From the first day they met he'd infuriated her, frustrated her, left her teary-eyed and somehow wedged himself firmly inside her heart.

After digging through the odds-and-ends drawer beneath her kitchen counter, she found the one thing she knew would soothe her. For the past two years she'd been a cross-stitch enthusiast. Not only did it appeal to her artistic side, but it helped her deal with stress. And her panic attacks. As she began making X shapes on the cloth, she found herself relaxing. She took a deep breath and then exhaled, closing her eyes and sending up a prayer to God.

A knock sounded at the back door, pulling her away from prayer and thoughts of Sawyer. Dolly and Casey were sitting at the counter snacking on grapes and playing rock, paper, scissors. Dolly slid down from her stool and ran toward the back door, answering the knock before Ava could admonish her about opening it before she knew who was outside. She pulled the door wide, and Sawyer was standing there in the doorway, his six-foot frame dwarfing her baby girl.

"You look like my daddy," Dolly announced in a voice filled with awe.

"Yeah, people used to tell me that all the time when I was growing up, but I never believed them," Sawyer said with a grin. "Do you remember me?"

"I think so," Dolly answered in a hesitant voice, turning toward Ava for reassurance. Ava nodded and smiled at her daughter, letting her know it was okay to talk to Sawyer.

"You're my uncle Sawyer!" Dolly said triumphantly. She reached for Sawyer's hand and pulled him over the threshold until he was standing inside the kitchen. Sawyer reached behind him and pushed the door closed.

Dolly's brown eyes went wide. "Mommy said you went away to the other side of the world. Casey said you weren't ever coming back, just like Daddy."

Ava's heart sank at the mournful tone in her daughter's voice. How in the world hadn't she known the twins had written Sawyer off as dead? Had she been so wrapped up in her own grief and pain she'd neglected to notice their losses, their suffering?

"I was gone for a long time," Sawyer acknowledged, looking over at Ava with eyes full of regret. "But I'm back now for good."

He reached out and tugged at one of Dolly's pigtails. She let out a squeal of excitement. When Sawyer held up his hand for a high five, Dolly slapped his palm with her own. Sawyer winced and shook his hand as if Dolly had hurt him. She beamed up at him, showcasing her missing front teeth.

Something inside Ava melted a little bit. The kids sorely needed a male presence in their lives. They would benefit by having their uncle Sawyer back in Cape Cod. Admitting her family needed him didn't change the slow burn eating its way through her.

"Casey. Come say hello to Uncle Sawyer," Ava said, noticing the way her son was studiously ignoring Sawyer. For a boy who never seemed to miss a thing, it was impossible to believe he was oblivious of Sawyer's arrival at their home. She suspected her son was playing possum.

Casey continued to sit at the table playing with his grapes, his eyes downcast. He made no attempt to get up from his stool or to speak to Sawyer.

"Casey!" Ava said in a warning tone. "Did you hear me?"

"Hey, buddy." Sawyer's tone was playful as he walked over to Casey. "How's it going?"

Finally, Casey looked up at Sawyer, his eyes glistening with an anger that made her want to wrap her arms around her son and soothe his heartbreak. He'd had so many losses in the past few years, too many to wrap his six-year-old head around. Everything he was feeling radiated from his eyes.

"You told us you'd be coming right back! You don't keep your promises," Casey shouted.

She saw Sawyer wince, and she knew Casey, in all his childish fury, had wounded him.

"Casey Trask!" Ava scolded. "You watch your tone of voice in this house. Apologize to your uncle."

Casey folded his arms across his chest. His lower lip stuck out in a pout. "I'm sorry," he apologized in a begrudging voice. "But you were gone for three hundred and forty-four days!" Casey announced. "That's almost a whole year."

"He marked it on a calendar." Dolly's tone was filled with pride. "And I helped him."

Ava's heart sank. Marking days on calendars? She'd had no idea the twins had been tracking Sawyer's absence. What kind of mother had she turned into over the past two years? Yes, in the beginning she'd been aware that they missed him terribly, but as the weeks turned into months they seemed almost indifferent to his absence. It was as if they'd forgotten him, and for some reason she hadn't done anything to solidify Sawyer's memory in their minds. She'd been so furious with him for leaving them, so incredibly wounded, a part of her had told herself Sawyer deserved to be forgotten. A feeling of shame trickled through her at the realization. After everything they'd been through together, she had owed him more than that.

"Do you two know what a mission is?" Sawyer asked the children. Both of them nodded, showing they didn't have a clue. "It's something very important that helps a lot of people," he explained. "That's what I was doing over in Africa. A lot of people were depending on me to help them."

"So you like those people better than you like us." Casey's arms were folded across his chest, and his words sounded accusatory.

"There's no one in this world I like better than the two of you." He bent down and went nose-to-nose with Casey. "I'm not going anywhere, Casey. I promise you. I'm back in town to stay."

"Prove it!" Casey demanded. "When I do something bad to Dolly, Mommy says the best way to show I'm sorry is by my actions."

Sawyer crossed his arms across his chest. "Oh, you want proof? Okay, come outside with me and I'll give you proof."

Sawyer quickly walked toward the back door, with Casey on his heels and Dolly trailing behind them. Filled with curiosity, Ava followed behind them, her interest piqued as Sawyer made his way to the edge of the property. He walked right up to the white picket fence that separated their property from the cliff and the beach down below. From this vantage point they had a bird's-eye view of miles and miles of ocean and the vast expanse of sandy beach.

Sawyer pointed in the direction of the lighthouse. "Do you know who lives there?" he asked the twins.

They both nodded. "That's Mr. P's house," Dolly chirped. "Except he went to Heaven."

Sawyer smiled. "Nope. That is not Mr. P's house. Not anymore."

Ava could see the confusion on the children's faces, and it mirrored her own bewilderment. What in the world was Sawyer trying to prove by bringing them outside and showing them the lighthouse? Casey and Dolly were still grappling with Mr. P's passing. She hoped there was a method to Sawyer's madness other than reminding the twins of yet another loss.

Sawyer stood there with his arms folded across his chest, a huge smile taking over his face. "I am now the proud owner of Mr. P's lighthouse."

"You mean you live there?" Casey asked, eyes wide with amazement.

He nodded enthusiastically, a pleased-with-himself grin etched on his face. "Yep. I live there, Casey. Right next door to you."

Ava let out a gasp of surprise. Right next door? Sawyer was the man she'd seen darting inside the lighthouse earlier. He was their new neighbor?

As the children jumped up and down in celebration, Ava felt goose bumps popping up on her arms. She wrapped her arms around her middle as she tried to process Sawyer's news. Living in such close proximity to him might prove to be problematic. Even though they'd once been best friends, a lot of water had flowed under the bridge since then. A part of her longed to go back to those days of innocence when their biggest problem had been coming up with enough money to go to the matinee.

She let out a soft sigh. So many things had changed between them since then, and for the life of her she didn't know how to get back to that place in time where they'd been able to finish each other's sentences and thumb wrestle for bragging rights. She didn't know how to get her best friend back.

Because no matter how hard she tried, Ava couldn't forget that one year ago they'd shared a tender kiss that had disturbed Sawyer so much he'd taken off for Africa the very next day.

Chapter Two

Fifteen minutes later they were all back inside the house. The twins were peppering him with questions about living in Africa and his coast guard mission. He'd already played a game of Uno with them, as well as one round of Scrabble and three rounds of hide-and-seek. As it neared dinnertime, they begged him to stay for dinner, oblivious of the fact that their mother didn't seem inclined to issue an invitation. With no shame, the twins took matters into their own hands.

"Mommy, can Uncle Sawyer stay for dinner?" Dolly asked, her hands crossed prayerfully in front of her.

"Can he? That would be so cool," Casey added. "He can tell us more about Africa."

"Please, please," they pleaded in unison.

Ava looked at the twins and nodded, a smile beginning to form at the corners of her mouth. Suddenly, she looked the way she used to, before her world had turned upside down.

Casey shouted, "Yes!" and high-fived his sister.

Sawyer was slightly amazed at his quick turnaround. An hour earlier Casey had been angrier than a hornet. Now, secure in the knowledge that his uncle Sawyer was sticking around, he was content.

He wished he could say the same about Casey's mother. Despite her smile, Ava's body language told a different story. She seemed tense and on edge. He had the feeling it had everything to do with his presence. When the kids scampered off to pick up their room before dinner, he moved toward the kitchen where Ava was cutting up vegetables for a salad.

"Anything I can do to help?" he offered. The silence between them was beginning to be uncomfortable. The beauty of their relationship had always rested in the easy flow of their conversations and the natural rhythms of their discussions. Ever since he could remember, Ava had been his sounding board, the one person he could always talk to about anything and everything. But something had shifted between them. Ever since he arrived at the house, he'd been itching to fill the empty space lying between them with conversation.

"No, I've got it. I'm just making a garden salad with some chicken stir-fry and jasmine rice." She didn't even bother to look up at him from her dinner preparations.

"You cut off all your hair." The words tumbled out of his mouth. For as long as he'd known Ava, her hair had trailed down her back. Now it was a sleek, shoulder-length bob. He stared at her, deciding that the short style suited her delicate features.

"It was too much of a hassle," she explained, wrinkling her nose. "With the kids in kindergarten now, I have to be out of the house by seven forty-five in order to make it to their school on time. We really hustle in the morning."

The thought of Ava and the kids bustling around the house in the morning tugged at his heart something fierce. Ever since Billy's death, she'd valiantly raised the twins and shouldered them through the mourning process. She'd stuffed down her own grief in order to help Casey and Dolly deal with their own fear and pain. According to his aunt Nancy, some nights Ava crumpled her body into their small twin beds and held them in her arms, determined to be there when the nightmares came. From what he'd witnessed firsthand, Ava Trask was an amazing mother.

"You never were a morning person, even when we were kids," Sawyer teased, wanting to see Ava let loose and relax. She seemed so tense, so ill at ease. He wasn't sure if it was because of everything she'd been through or because of him.

"When you become a parent you don't really have a choice," she explained. "You just have to learn how to adapt, otherwise the kids would be late for school every day and I'd never get anything done around here."

"If you don't mind my saying so, you seem less than thrilled about my moving next door," Sawyer said with a grimace.

She was standing at the kitchen counter dicing green peppers, onions and carrots. Every time the knife hit the cutting block, he winced. She seemed to be on edge and had been avoiding eye contact with him. The vegetables seemed to be taking a beating.

Ava shrugged. "Sawyer, the kids are over the moon about it, so I'm thankful for their sakes."

"But not your own?" He studied her expression carefully, picking up on her reservations by her pursed lips and the awkward tilt of her head.

She sighed. "I didn't say that. It's just that we haven't seen you for a year, and then you turn up on the beach having just bought the lighthouse next door." She let out a shaky laugh. "You have to admit, it's a little unexpected."

"Ava, you know how I feel about Mr. P's lighthouse. I've loved it since the first time I saw it." He studied her expression, wondering if she remembered all the times Mr. P had invited them over to his lighthouse when they were kids. He'd been amazing to them, as generous and kind as one could imagine. Between playing pirate, teaching them to catch crabs and watching old movies with them, he'd played the role of grandfather in their lives. He'd taught Sawyer what it meant to be part of a community and how to establish bonds that lasted a lifetime.

"Is it odd to want to help out my family?"

"No, not at all." She let out a sigh. "But I don't want to rely on someone who—"

"Who bailed on you?" he said in a gruff tone. "Just say it."

She finally looked straight at him. "What the twins need most of all is consistency. I'm not trying to make you feel bad, but when you left it took us a long time to get back to normal."

As they locked gazes, tension crackled in the air between them. Ava looked away, focusing instead on the cutting board. "After Billy died, you were our rock. You did so much for us. No matter what, I'll always be grateful for that." Midway through, her voice became husky with emotion. "Other than my sisters, you were there for us like nobody else."

"Why is it so hard to look at me, Ava? Are you still that angry at me?" he asked in a gentle voice. "Am I still unforgiven?"

She looked at him, her hazel eyes brimming with emotion. She slammed her palm down on the counter. Her graceful hands were shaking. "Why? Because the last time the two of us were alone together you kissed me. And the very next day you were packing for Africa, as if you couldn't wait to get as far away from me as humanly possible. And for the past year I've been blaming myself for my kids losing yet another person they love."

Did she really just bring up that ill-fated kiss? That sweet, tender kiss he'd been trying to forget for a whole year?

Although the kiss had been at the forefront of his mind ever since he'd left for Africa, he'd never expected Ava to mention it. It was a sore subject for him. He felt as if he'd crossed a line by kissing her, and he'd been second-guessing himself ever since. For so long now he'd thought of her as Billy's wife, as far out of reach as a constellation in the sky. His feelings had always been under the radar until that life-altering moment when he'd acted on impulse and pressed his lips against hers.

And because she'd still been knee-deep in mourning, he'd never wanted Ava to think he was trying to take advantage of a grief-stricken widow. Their twenty-five-year friendship meant too much to him to risk losing.

"That kiss was impulsive," he admitted, choosing his words carefully. "We'd been spending so much time together, day in, day out. We were both grieving for Billy." He shrugged. "It should never have happened."

"Was it why you left?" she asked. Her eyes were beseeching him to be straight with her. "Please, be honest with me. I feel like everything shifted between us after that night. And then you were gone. I lost my best friend." There was so much vulnerability in her voice. It made him want to reach out to her, to put his arms around her and shelter her from all her doubts. But he couldn't do that, no matter how much he wanted to hold her. There were still too many things he'd never come clean about.

"No, Ava. It wasn't the reason I left. The mission in Sierra Leone was a lot more important than a random kiss. Please don't blame yourself." As far as the truth was concerned, he hadn't told her any lies. The kiss hadn't been the sole reason he'd accepted the Africa assignment. There had been other factors, things he didn't want to lay at her feet. He knew he was minimizing the kiss, but he couldn't admit to Ava what it had meant to him. If he did, nothing between them would ever be the same. The last thing he wanted to do was complicate her life, to make her grieving process any more difficult. As it was, their friendship seemed to be hanging on by a thread.

"And for the record, you could never lose me. Not in a million years." He felt a warmth spreading in his chest as his own sentiments rolled over him. She meant the world to him. How could she not know that? Had his overseas mission caused her to doubt what they'd always meant to each other? Ava's face tensed up for a second, and then she seemed to relax. He watched as she let out a deep sigh.

Dear Lord, forgive me for bending the truth about the kiss. The last thing I want to do is hurt Ava, to put her on the spot by telling her that after our kiss I needed to get as far away from her as possible. Because the truth is I was starting to fall head over heels for my cousin's widow, and I couldn't handle the guilt. So I did the only thing that made sense at the time. I put a world of distance between us.

He'd learned a year ago that pushing for something more with Ava was unfair. His feelings for her had always been deep and powerful, ever since they were kids. Although they'd been best buddies growing up, deep down he'd always felt something special between them. When he'd left Cape Cod to attend the Coast Guard Academy and she'd started dating Billy, it had been a harsh blow to recover from. He'd kept quiet, though, never letting Ava know he was hurt and jealous. In his mind she would forever be the one who'd gotten away. Many times he'd asked God to grant him the grace to accept that Ava had chosen Billy as her life partner. Many times he'd knelt before God and prayed for his feelings to disappear. And for many years he'd believed that what he felt for Ava was buried so deep down that no one ever suspected a thing. Until that terrible night when Billy had called him out and accused him of wanting Ava for himself. Until tragedy had altered all of their lives.

"So, we're good?" Ava asked, a slight frown furrowing her brow.

He reached across the butcher block counter and reached for her hand. Her hand was soft and supple, radiating warmth. It felt so good to be touching her, connecting with her. He couldn't even put into words how much he'd missed her. "We're good," he said with a nod. "Better than good."

The noisy clatter of the children heralded their arrival in the kitchen. Sawyer quickly pulled his hand away, and Ava placed her hands on the counter. "Three minutes to dinner," she announced in a breathy voice. "Why don't the two of you head to the sink and wash up?"

Dolly looked up at him. "Don't you have to get washed up, too? Kids aren't the only ones with germy hands."

Sawyer let loose with a hearty chuckle. He'd missed the twins' blunt outlook on life. He'd missed being able to laugh out loud. There hadn't been much to laugh about in Sierra Leone, although he'd bonded with the local children and learned a lot about their culture. Although a coast guard presence in the region had been crucial, it had been a personal hardship to be over there for such a long time.

"I won't give you any argument about that, Miss Dolly," he answered. "Ladies first." He bent over and waved his hand in the air as if she were royalty. Dolly raced by him toward the kitchen sink, followed closely by Casey. He joined them, passing by their refrigerator decorated with artwork and family photos. A heart-shaped magnet said God Bless This Home. When he spotted a photo of himself standing next to Billy, both of them holding a twin in their arms, he found himself getting choked up. He remembered the moment vividly. It was the day of their baptism, and as honorary uncle to both of the twins, he'd proudly posed for a picture with his cousin.

"If anything happens to me, I want you to watch over Casey and Dolly. You're the closest thing to a brother I have, and I want my kids to know you as Uncle Sawyer." Billy's words came flooding back to him. Guilt seized him by the throat. He'd let Billy down. He hadn't watched over the twins. Not for the past year anyway. He'd been too busy running away—from his feelings, from his guilt, from his pain, from that unforgettable kiss. The memory of Billy's words had been part of the reason he'd come back earlier than planned. He had a responsibility to the twins, not only as their honorary uncle, but because of the heartfelt wish Billy had expressed to him on that day.

And no matter what happened from this point forward, he was going to uphold his promise, even though it would place him in direct contact with Ava.

As they settled in around the dinner table, Ava had to admit to herself that she felt happier than she had in quite some time. Seeing the kids so overjoyed about

Sawyer's return made her feel grateful. And if she was being honest, she had to admit she felt some stirrings within her own soul. For so long now she'd felt a little frozen, as if nothing could penetrate the shield she'd placed around her heart. Even though she was a bit embarrassed about lashing out at Sawyer, at least she'd felt a strong emotion. At least she'd felt something other than numbness. For the first time in a long while, she felt alive.

No matter what issues stood between them, she was thankful Sawyer had made it back safe and sound. From the little she knew about Sierra Leone, it was a dangerous place. Civil wars, violence and disease were an everyday part of life there. Although she knew the coast guard had important missions to conduct, she was relieved Sawyer would be out of the line of fire. The thought of losing another person she loved was too painful to even consider. She didn't want to think about Sawyer being gone from her world. Especially since he'd just come back to them.

"Who wants to say grace?" Sawyer asked. He looked around the table, going from one face to the next. The twins looked at each other with a baffled expression and shrugged their shoulders.

Her cheeks flushed with embarrassment. "We don't always say grace," she admitted. "We've gotten out of the habit."

Sawyer looked taken aback for a moment, but he quickly recovered as he extended his hands to the twins, who were seated on either side of him. She reached out and clasped hands with Casey and Dolly so that they formed a circle of four. She bowed her head, hoping Sawyer would take the lead and say Grace. Although she knew the words by heart, she was afraid she would stumble over the blessing.

"Dear Lord," Sawyer began in a strong, steady voice, "we offer thanks for this wonderful meal, lovingly prepared by Ava. We thank you for the abundant gifts you bestow on us each and every day. Thank you for watching over this family and for guiding me safely back home where I belong. Amen."

"Amen," she said in unison with the children. Hearing Sawyer's blessing caused a warm heat to spread through her chest. It meant the world to her that she and the kids were in his thoughts and prayers. Somehow it made her feel safe and protected. It had been a long time since she'd felt that way.

They all dug into the stir-fry, enjoying a companionable silence as they ate. Having Sawyer sit down to a meal with her family seemed to be a big hit with the twins. Neither of them could take their eyes off him. He was the main attraction. It was amazing how quickly they'd taken him back into their hearts, considering the length of time he'd been away. There was no trace of Casey's earlier resentment. Resilience. Kids were known for being able to bounce back, weren't they? Sometimes she forgot that their little hearts were stronger than she could ever imagine.

"Uncle Sawyer," Dolly said in a garbled voice. "Are you coming to the wedding?"

"Dolly, it might be more polite to talk without the food in your mouth," Ava cautioned. Her daughter's cheeks were stuffed to the brim, causing her to resemble a squirrel storing acorns.

Dolly's eyes got big, and she made a dramatic effort at swallowing her food. She then reached for her glass of water and took a few sips. "Uncle Sawyer," she repeated. "Are you coming to the wedding?"

Sawyer's lips twitched with amusement. "Cousin Melanie's wedding?" Dolly nodded her head enthusiastically. Growing up in a sea of boy cousins, Melanie had always occupied a special place in all of their hearts. Sawyer treated Dolly to a full-fledged smile. "I wouldn't miss it for the world, even though I just heard about it yesterday." He frowned. "Who's this guy she's fallen so madly in love with?"

"His name is Doug, and he's awesome," Casey raved, his brown eyes glittering with excitement. "He's got a motorcycle and everything."

"I get to be a flower girl," Dolly shouted. "And I have a pretty new dress to wear."

Casey stuck his lip out. "And I get to be the ring boy."

Dolly snorted with laughter and covered her mouth with her hand. "It's ring bearer, Casey," she sputtered. Casey shot her a dirty look and jabbed her in the side. Dolly retaliated, beginning a back-and-forth war that threatened to get out of control. Ava wondered if her face betrayed her exasperation. Lately, more times than not, Casey and Dolly couldn't get through a meal without invading each other's personal space and getting on one another's nerves, as well as her own.

"Who wants to hear a story about your mom when she was around your age?" Sawyer asked smoothly, diverting the kids' attention from their squabble. Casey and Dolly jumped on the opportunity, and, in the process, forgot all about their feud. Ava was slightly in awe. Sawyer had serious skills. He'd thrown the question out there like a perfectly aimed pitch. The kids had never even seen it coming. They were sitting quietly, waiting expectantly for the story to begin.

"Well, when I moved to Buzzards Bay, I didn't have a single friend in my class." He looked back and forth between the twins. "Rough, huh?"

"Not a single one?" Dolly asked, her eyes wide with concern. "What about my daddy?"

He shook his head. "Nope. Your dad was a few grades above me, so I was pretty much on my own."

"I would have been your friend," Casey piped up, shooting Sawyer a doting smile.

Sawyer reached out and patted Casey on the shoulder. "I'm sure you would have."

Even though Ava knew what was coming next, she found herself listening to Sawyer with rapt attention. It was entertaining to see the expectant looks on the children's faces and to hear the details of their first meeting roll off Sawyer's tongue like quicksilver.

"On the first day of school I forgot my lunch at home," Sawyer continued. He wiggled his eyebrows dramatically. "Can you imagine? There I was, in the lunchroom with no one to sit with and no homemade lunch to dig into. I didn't even have a juice box."

Casey and Dolly turned toward each other, their eyes as wide as saucers. In their lives, juice boxes were as routine as the sun rising in the morning.

"I looked all around the cafeteria until I found the perfect lunch table to sit at. Problem was, everyone else was eating their lunches. I was so embarrassed I could barely lift my head up to make eye contact as I slid onto the bench. For a few minutes I just sat there, wishing I could disappear. All of a sudden this little hand reached across the table and handed me half of her sandwich. Peanut butter and jelly never tasted quite so good."

"Was that you, Mama?" Dolly asked, her eyes full of wonder.

"Yep. It was me," Ava acknowledged. "And I also gave him a cookie and half of my pretzels."

The poignant memory washed over her like a light rain, and for a moment she was transported back in time to Buzzards Bay Elementary and sitting across the lunch table from a pint-size Sawyer. The grateful smile he'd given her after she'd offered him the sandwich had quickly wormed its way straight into her heart. And he'd been there ever since, engraved there like a permanent tattoo.

Sawyer winked at her, almost as if he could read her mind. "And from that moment on we were best friends. We did everything together...we built forts in the woods, swam out to the buoys at Kalmus Beach, had water balloon fights, took ferry rides over to Woods Hole."

"We keep asking to take a boat ride in one of the boats by the harbor, but Mommy says we can't," Casey added, casting an unhappy look in her direction. "She thinks something might happen to us." His eyes were hot with displeasure and a hint of rebelliousness.

Ava felt the heat of Sawyer's gaze, but she didn't look over at him. As a man who made his living by enforcing maritime law, he might find it difficult to understand her fears. For Sawyer, being out on the water was as natural as breathing. Casey was right. The thought of her kids being out on the water scared her to death. Some might call it an irrational fear, but it was rooted in that awful night two years ago when her husband hadn't come home.

"Why don't the two of you clear the table and feed Tully?" Ava asked. "Then I'll slice up some apple pie for dessert." The mention of dessert sweetened the deal, causing the kids to quickly get up from their seats and begin clearing the dinner plates.

"It'll be nice to have all the family together to celebrate a happy occasion," Ava said as soon as the kids were out of earshot. "Too many times we've gathered for sad ones." Truthfully, she had mixed feelings about attending a wedding in the same church where she'd married Billy. It would dredge up a lot of bittersweet memories, she realized. She felt a stab of guilt as she remembered all the times she'd seen happily-in-love couples over the past two years. Whether they were holding hands on the beach or grocery shopping at the market, she'd envied them their bliss. It had been that way between Billy and her, hadn't it? Before all the drinking and the stormy fights, the recriminations and the promises. Hadn't people looked at them and thought how blessed they were to have found each other? Hadn't she once believed they were golden?

"You're right," Sawyer said with a nod. "Our families have had our fair share of loss. It's been a rough couple of years." He crinkled his nose. "Even so, I'm a firm believer that we're always surrounded by blessings. Sometimes we just have to look closely to find them."

Blessings. Sawyer was right. Despite everything, there was so much in her life to be thankful about. The twins. Her home by the sea. Her family. Sawyer. "How do you do it?" she asked with a grateful sigh. "You always manage to put things into such beautiful perspective."

He shrugged, his expression thoughtful. "I just spent a year watching kids kick empty soda cans around instead of soccer balls. And guess what? They were joyful about it. Amid poverty and destruction, those kids were able to see the good things in their world."

The soft shuffling of little feet and the noisy squeak of a floorboard heralded the arrival of the twins. Casey stood a few feet away from the table, a huge grin almost overtaking his small, round face. Dolly stood two steps behind him, none too subtly nudging him forward and whispering in his ear. Sawyer beckoned them closer with a wave of his hand. "Come on. I can see the two of you have something to say."

"Dolly and I thought maybe we could visit you at the Coast Guard Station one day. We promise to be on our best behavior." The worshipful expression in Casey's eyes as he looked up at Sawyer caused her to suck in a shallow breath. The raw need in his voice almost knocked the wind out of her. It sneaked up on her during quiet moments like this when she saw the hopes and dreams of her children put on full display. Her son so needed a father figure in his life, someone who could keep up with his rough-and-tumble ways. Someone he could model himself after. Gratitude toward Sawyer for being here with them flooded through her.

"We promise not to get in the way," Dolly piped up. Her hands were crossed tightly in front of her. Her hazel eyes radiated hopefulness. And pleading. Ava clucked to herself, knowing Sawyer was no match against the dynamic duo.

"I think that can be arranged," he said with a pearl-toothed smile. He shot a glance in her direction. "As long as it's all right with your mom."

Dolly and Casey shifted their gaze toward her. She quickly nodded, signaling her approval. The twins began dancing around the room in celebratory fashion. Within seconds they were racing out of the room to feed the dog, their voices raised in triumph. She let out a chuckle and playfully looked at her watch. "Hmm. Less than two hours in their presence, and you're already caving in to their wishes. At this rate they're going to have you wrapped around their little fingers in no time."

"I want the twins to be happy," he said with a poignant smile. "And I want that for you, too, Ava."

She swallowed past the huge lump in her throat. "I am happy. Most of the time. Until I think about Billy," she said in a quiet voice. "It's a terrible thing to have to always think about the way he died and not be able to celebrate the way he lived his life. I still can't wrap my head around being a widow before I've even turned thirty."

Sawyer reached out and grazed his knuckles across

her cheek, his eyes full of compassion. And understanding. Sawyer knew her so well. He always had. For most of her life he'd been her soft place to fall, the one person she ran to when the bottom fell out of her world. But that had changed when she'd married Billy. Neither one of them had felt comfortable with that type of closeness once she became Mrs. Billy Trask. She'd always been well aware of the fact that Billy was jealous of her relationship with Sawyer. Having such a tight bond with him had made her feel disloyal. In the end she'd pulled away from him, breaking her own heart a little in the process.

And now, once again, she felt traitorous. To Billy. To their children. Yet it felt so nice to be connecting with Sawyer, to enjoy his warm palm against her cheek. To feel as if there was someone who knew her better than she knew herself. It felt too good. She didn't deserve comfort or sympathy. She'd failed Billy in the biggest way possible. As a wife, as a friend and as a mother of his children. Not even Sawyer knew the extent of her failures as a wife. He had no idea that she'd been complicit in her husband's death. She could only imagine his disgust if he knew how she'd nagged at Billy until he'd left their home the night of his accident. If not for that, her husband would still be alive.

She abruptly pulled away from Sawyer, immediately feeling the loss of his touch. She smoothed her hair back and looked away from his probing gaze, trying to appear calm despite the turbulent emotions she was battling. Ever since that tantalizing kiss with Sawyer she'd had to remind herself that it wasn't wise to risk their friendship over tender kisses and comforting caresses. She couldn't run the risk of losing him all over again. It had gutted her when he left for Africa. Although it hurt to pull away from something that nurtured her very soul, she had no choice in the matter. Because the one person who could soothe her restless soul was the very person she was determined not to fall for.

After two slices of delectable apple pie and two rounds of Go Fish, Sawyer stood up and announced his departure. He couldn't help smiling when Casey and Dolly begged him to stay longer. This was what he'd missed in Africa, he realized. A sense of belonging.

"Please, just a little bit longer," they pleaded. With a loud groan, Ava peeled the children off him as they clung tightly to his legs.

He leaned on the counter to keep his balance. "I'll be back soon, guys. I promise. I have to run over to my parents' house tomorrow and then head in to work, but the next day we can meet up, maybe at the coast guard station."

Ava looked at him curiously. "So, no one in the family mentioned you were back in town," she said.

Sawyer grimaced. "That's because you guys are the first to know other than my team. I wanted to take care of a few things before I announced my return."

Ava grinned, her face lit up like sunshine. "Such as buying a lighthouse?"

He nodded. "Yep. Like buying a lighthouse." He moved his hand to his jaw and rubbed it. "It didn't hit me till now, but my folks just might wonder about my sanity."

She stopped grinning. Her eyes wandered over his face. "No, they won't. They're going to be so over the moon that you're back, they won't care if you're living in a shack on the beach."

He felt a warmth spreading through his veins as Ava's words settled in. "Well, then, I'm off," he said as he made his way to the back door. Casey trailed right behind him while Dolly blew him kisses. Once he was outside he heard Ava calling out to him, her voice pulling him right back toward her. He turned back, watching as she practically flew out of the house straight toward him. Once again he noticed how radiant she looked. And much more relaxed than the Ava he'd first encountered on the beach earlier today. He was thankful she'd forgiven him, or at least had decided to give him a second chance to be in her life. He felt himself smiling at the notion that something he'd done—some little word or gesture—had made her happy tonight.

"I never said welcome back." She walked toward him, reaching him in a few short strides. She stood on her tiptoes and leaned up toward him, placing a tender kiss on his cheek. Ava smiled at him—the first jubilant smile she'd given him since he'd seen her. With a wave of her hand, she headed back toward the house.

The smile went straight to his heart, reminding him of all the reasons he'd left Cape Cod and found refuge on the other side of the world. He'd thought he was strong enough to come back home and face the past, but all of a sudden he was doubting himself. Now that he was standing here in her orbit, he wasn't so sure that he could bury his feelings and man up.

You don't have a choice. The words buzzed in his ear. After all, this was about the children, not about him. That's why he'd come back, wasn't it?

As Ava walked back into the house, he watched through the window as the twins rushed toward her to give her a hug. The sight of it caused him to let out a deep shudder. What would it be like to be part of that tight-knit family unit? he wondered. What would it be like to tuck the kids into bed at night and see them off to school in the morning? He shook the thought off, chastising himself for allowing his mind to go down that road. This was Billy's family, not his. No matter how strongly he felt for them, for Ava, it was disloyal to Billy to even let his mind go there. When he'd kissed Ava that night, he'd been full of remorse and guilt afterward. So much self-recrimination. What kind of man would he be if he took up with his cousin's widow?

As if that could ever happen! She wouldn't want to have anything to do with him if she knew the truth, he realized. Because of him, Ava's husband and the father of her twins had drowned off Nantucket Sound. And no matter what Sawyer did to assuage the guilt, it still gnawed at him. In his career he'd saved a hundred lives or more, nearly losing his own half a dozen times in the process. A few of his rescues had been recoveries, but none of them had haunted him like Billy's death. None of them had given him nightmares that had him crying out in the middle of the night.

The memories of that night washed over him like

a tidal wave as he walked along the beach toward his lighthouse.

He and Billy had owned a boat leasing company. It had been Billy's idea, and he had gone along with it, knowing that his cousin needed something to focus on since he'd been laid off from his job. Billy was supposed to be doing most of the work during the week, while Sawyer chipped in on weekends during his off time. Much to his dismay, he'd found himself doing the lion's share of the work, and he'd resented it. They'd formed the business out of their mutual love for boats, but all the joy had vanished. He'd sunk a lot of money into Trask Boating, and it annoyed him that they hadn't even been able to get it off the ground because of Billy's lackadaisical attitude.

As usual, Billy had shown up two hours late and inebriated. The smell of cheap liquor clung to his cousin like a second skin. Sawyer had confronted him, sick and tired of picking up the slack for the business they were trying to get up and running. The company was hanging on by a thread owing to his financial contribution, and he had been starting to feel that Billy was taking advantage of him.

"You owe Ava and the twins better than this!" he'd said after chastising his cousin for drinking.

"Don't tell me about my family! What do you know about keeping a marriage together or raising kids? The last time I checked you're still single. Footloose and fancy free."

"You're right about that," he'd acknowledged. "But if the good Lord ever blesses me with a wonderful wife like Ava, I'd treat her a sight better than you're doing at the moment."

Right before his eyes, Billy's face had hardened into granite. His eyes had narrowed into slits. He'd began clenching his fists. An angry vein had popped on his forehead.

"You'd like that, wouldn't you? A wife like Ava. Maybe Ava herself would do, right? Ava and Sawyer. You like the ring of that, don't you?"

"Stop, Billy. You're out of line."

Billy had brushed up against him and gotten in his face. "Am I? It seems to me that you don't think I'm good enough for my own wife. Is that it?"

He'd held up his hands, knowing that once Billy got started on a tangent he was a tough person to try to wind down. "Stop playing the victim in this. It's not about that."

"You stop, Sawyer. Stop judging me. Stop throwing everything in my face. Stop wishing that Ava was married to you instead of me!"

Billy's words had almost knocked the wind out of him. He'd opened his mouth to refute the accusation, determined to deny he'd been holding on to any romantic notions about him and Ava. As much as he'd wanted to deny it, he couldn't. He'd let out a deep sigh. "Yes, I have wished Ava was mine. And I want you to know I've always been ashamed of that. Until right now. Because seeing you like this, watching you destroy the wonderful life you've built for yourself—" He'd stopped for a moment, too overcome with frustration to continue. "And let me tell you, if she were my wife, I'd treat her a whole lot better than you've been treating her lately."

The words hung in the air like a storm cloud on the verge of bursting. For a moment the room was quiet, with nothing more than tension crackling in the air.

"No wonder she keeps nagging me," Billy had muttered. "How can I compare to the great hero, Sawyer Trask? So perfect and righteous."

"Don't call me that, Billy!" he'd growled, wishing it didn't get under his skin so much when people touted him as a hero. In his mind he wasn't a hero. He was an officer in the coast guard, sworn to uphold maritime law. Performing search-and-rescues was just part and parcel of his job duties. He wasn't anybody's hero!

"Always so noble," Billy had spit out. "It must be nice to be perfect." He'd shaken his head in disgust. "I'm out of here!" he'd shouted, his long legs quickly carrying him to the door. Those were the last words they'd ever spoken to each other.

A hundred times or more since that night, Sawyer had wished he'd stopped Billy from leaving. It was the last time he'd seen his cousin alive. Late that night he'd received the call from a frantic Ava, who hadn't seen or heard from her husband all evening. For hours he'd driven around town looking for his cousin, to no avail. In the wee hours of the morning he'd received the devastating call from his best friend, Colby, who was a member of his coast guard unit. Billy's capsized boat had been spotted by the coast guard a few miles out in the harbor. Although everyone had prayed that he'd managed to swim to land, Billy's body had been found the next day in one of the inlets off Buzzards Bay Harbor. An investigation had concluded that, caught in a minor squall, Billy had drowned after his boat took on water. The fact that Billy had been under the influence had only worsened the life-and-death situation.

Sawyer had never told a single soul about his argument with Billy. He'd been too ashamed, felt too guilty about the fact that his angry words with him might have caused his cousin to spiral downward. But he couldn't keep this to himself any longer. Not when he'd made a promise to God he'd come clean with Ava after he'd almost died from cholera on the other side of the world.

Chapter Three

As Sawyer drove down Seaview Avenue, he felt a strong sense of nostalgia sweep over him. With his window down he could smell the tangy scent of the ocean as it permeated the air. The high-pitched cries of a flock of seagulls drifted toward him from the beach. The pink gingerbread-style house that sat on the corner of Seaview Avenue and Ocean Street had been there for as long as he could remember. He tooted his horn and waved at the owner, Mrs. Kingston, who was outside watering her rosebushes. She squinted at first, then began to wave enthusiastically as soon as she recognized him. Yes, this was what he'd yearned for while he was overseas. Home. Hearth. A feeling of being connected to his community.

He began to slow his Jeep down as the Trask home came into view, its bright yellow color a departure from the classic Cape Cod–style homes surrounding it. The historic house was built by his great-great-grandfather, sea captain Adam Trask, for his young bride. He'd built a widow's walk on the second floor so that his bride could look out to sea for his return. His parents had lovingly restored the home when his father had inherited it some thirty years earlier.

Sawyer parked his car in the driveway and made his way to the front door. It swung open well before he even planted a foot on the front porch. His father, Samuel, was standing at the door, a perplexed look plastered on his face. He was tall and broad-shouldered, with a barrel chest that spoke of strength. He'd been told on more than one occasion about their shared resemblance—the same caramel skin, full brows and deep set eyes. "Well, come on in, son. We were wondering when you were going to show up," his father drawled as he pushed open the door and ushered him inside.

Sawyer felt a sinking sensation in the pit of his stomach as he stepped inside the house and came face-to-face with his mother. Was he about to get a tongue lashing for not immediately coming to the house after his arrival in Buzzards Bay? The moment he saw her, his spirits lifted. After all this time away from home, she was a sight for sore eyes. At barely five feet, she was petite and small boned. Despite her salt-and-pepper hair, she still looked at least ten years younger than her actual age.

At the moment her pretty face was marred by a deep scowl. She placed her hands on her hips. "You've been back in town for three days without a word or a call. Nothing!" His mother slashed her hand in the air for emphasis. "Sawyer Trask! I know I've raised you better than that!"

He should have known, he thought miserably. In a small town like Buzzards Bay, it was near impossible to keep a secret. As much as he'd thought he could pull it off, word of his arrival had already reached his mother's ears. So much for his coast guard training in stealth maneuvers!

"Mom, I'm so sorry," he apologized. "I should have come straight to the house. Or at least called to tell you I was back." He held up his arms to give her a hug, but she pushed him away.

She looked him over with a critical eye. "You're so thin," she said. "What were they feeding you over there?"

Of course his mother noticed his weight loss. With her eagle eye and attention to detail, it wasn't surprising that she would see what others didn't. He'd lost twelve pounds during his bout with cholera, most of which he'd put back on in the months afterward. He was still down five pounds or so. His parents had no idea that he'd contracted cholera and had hovered near death for almost a week. By the time he was on the mend, he hadn't seen the point in telling them about his brush with death. It would only have made them worry about him more, he'd realized. And, despite the risks he frequently assumed in his profession, he didn't want his parents to lie awake at night thinking about his safety. They had enough to worry about with his younger brother, Daniel.

"I ate plenty over there," he said with a grin. "Nothing that could compare to your home cooking, but it was decent." He leaned down and wrapped his long arms around her, lifting her slightly off the floor in the process. She let out a little squeal and ordered him to let her down. When he placed her back down, he planted a kiss on her cheek. The sweet smell of home lingered around her like perfume—the scent of baked apples, cider doughnuts and cinnamon all reminded him of growing up in this loving environment. Warm hugs and down-home cooking came to mind.

Like a whirlwind, his brother, Daniel, came crashing down the stairs. Tall, broad-shouldered and thick, he headed straight for Sawyer, enveloping him in a bear hug that nearly toppled him over. As usual, his enthusiasm was off the charts.

"You're back! I knew it, I knew it." Daniel kept him in a tight grip until Sawyer had to practically wrestle his brother in order to come up for air. He put his arm around Daniel and pulled him close. Even though Daniel was twenty years old, he had the childlike nature of a ten-year-old. He was a kind and gentle soul who was often misunderstood because of his developmental disability. People tended to judge him by his physical age and were taken aback by his stunted emotional development.

"Hey, I promised I'd be back by Fourth of July, didn't I? I'm a month early," Sawyer pointed out, holding up his palm so Daniel could high-five him.

His father frowned at him. "Where are you staying, son? I know you gave up your condo when you left the country, so I imagine you're looking for a new place."

"We've got plenty of room here if you need a place to rest your head." His mother winked at him. "We won't even charge you rent if you wash a few dishes now and then."

He rocked back on his heels, his hands stuffed in his front pockets. There was no point in waiting any longer to tell his parents about his new accommodations. He cleared his throat. "Well, I have some news. I bought Mr. P's lighthouse. It's my new home."

"That is so cool!" Daniel shouted. "I can't wait to sleep over at your house." He started jumping up and down with excitement and pumping his fists in the air.

His parents exchanged a knowing look. His mother's lips were pursed. His father was stroking his chin, a contemplative look etched on his face.

"What? Is there something wrong with that?" Sawyer asked, suddenly feeling defensive. "You two look pretty grim."

His mother shrugged. "No, there's nothing wrong with it. It's your decision, son. But I do have a question for you. Does this decision to buy the lighthouse have to do with Ava and the kids?"

Sawyer pulled at his ear. He detected a hint of disapproval in his parents' attitude. He let out a huff of air. "I made a promise to Billy that I would watch over the twins. Not being able to do that over the past year…" His voice trailed off as emotion took over. "I feel like I let Ava and the kids down. Now I'm close enough to really be of help to Ava."

The expression on his father's face was a mixture of shock and dismay. "You've gone to great lengths to keep your promise to your cousin. Don't you think buying the lighthouse is a bit excessive?"

"Not at all. What you're forgetting is that I've always wanted to live in the lighthouse," he reasoned, his tone firm and decisive. "You know how I used to go on and on about it when I was a kid. By buying Mr. P's house I can accomplish two goals at the same time."

His parents still looked baffled. He caught his mother discreetly nudging his father in the side, and he knew a lecture was about to commence.

"That's all very honorable, son. It says a lot about who you are as a person," his father acknowledged. "But we just think it's high time you started building your own family. If you focus too much on Billy's family, how will you ever find time for a personal life? It's time you meet a nice girl and settle down." His voice sounded soothing yet firm.

The beginnings of a smile tugged at the corners of Sawyer's mouth. He had this conversation with his parents every few months or so. Even though he wasn't yet thirty, they wanted their son to be married with children and living in domestic bliss. They wanted to bounce grandchildren on their knees. A random image of Ava fluttered through his mind, and he forced himself to shake it away.

"Helping them out won't get in the way of a personal life," he insisted. He glanced back and forth between his parents. Something didn't feel right about this conversation. He felt as if he was missing some crucial piece of information. "Why do I have the feeling something else is going on?"

Again, his parents shared a private look. "Your uncle Troy is a little sensitive about you and Ava spending so much time together," his mother explained in a low voice. She paused for a moment. "He thinks it doesn't look right. Before you left for Africa, he made it clear it was an issue for him. We didn't have the heart to tell you, especially since you'd been so supportive to Ava and the kids."

Uncle Troy was his father's brother, as well as being Billy's dad, and they'd always been the best of friends. A stab of guilt pierced him at the thought that his actions had created tension within the family. After all, they'd all been through so much. Although Uncle Troy had spoken to him about his objections, he'd had no idea the topic had been broached with his parents. "We're just friends, Ava and I. That's all we've ever been, ever since we were kids." He threw his hands up in the air. He was battling against a rising sense of irritation. "I can't believe this is a problem. Ava and I were friends long before she married Billy."

His words hung in the air for a moment like a live grenade. He probably came across as sounding petty, as if he were a kid on the playground arguing over territory. He knew he was acting defensive, but it annoyed him to no end the way his family minimized his long-standing friendship with Ava. They acted as if he didn't have his own relationship with her outside of Billy. On some level he felt as if everyone in the family was dancing around the fact that he and Ava shared an unbreakable bond. Didn't his feelings matter at all?

"Son, you've been an amazing support system for Ava and the kids. And of course, we all know the depth of your friendship." He patted Sawyer on the back. "I

don't see why you shouldn't continue to be there for
them. We all love them. But I have to admit I do worry
about the strain it will cause within the family. Troy
and Nancy have already suffered the loss of their only
child. We just don't want to add to it. Family has to stick
together." His rich voice was filled with emotion, and
Sawyer knew his father was torn between his brother's
wishes, his own son's needs and what might be right
for Ava's family.

But he wasn't going to give his father a free pass.
He couldn't believe what he'd just heard tumbling from
his lips. Family has to stick together? Had his father really said that? Wasn't Ava part of his extended family?
And wasn't he honoring his cousin's bequest by standing by Billy's family?

"The last time I checked, Ava and the twins are part
of this family, too." Try as he might, he couldn't manage to keep the anger out of his voice.

Needing to cool off, he walked outside where he
found Daniel kicking around a soccer ball. He joined
in, knowing that spending time with his brother was
the best cure for his current mood. Hearing his parents
voice their concerns hit him hard. They were forcing
him to think about all the reasons he could never be
with Ava. It wasn't as if he hadn't already harbored
these doubts, but hearing someone put them into words
served as a brutal reminder.

He knew if he pursued Ava, it might tear his family
apart. They would never accept a relationship between
the two of them. It would be perceived as the ultimate
betrayal of Billy. Uncle Troy had told him as much right

before he'd left for Africa. He'd never told his parents about the argument they'd had and the way his uncle had blown up at him. He'd accused him of moving in on Billy's widow and of taking advantage of her grief-stricken state. He'd already been filled with remorse after kissing Ava that night, so his uncle's words later that evening had hit him in a tender spot. The fact that he and Billy had been competing with each other their whole lives only served to heighten his guilt.

Being near Ava and having such intense feelings for her had been too much to bear. At the time he'd found it impossible to be in her presence day after day, all the while knowing that she was out of reach. It was agony not being able to tell her how he felt. When he'd received the call from his commanding officer about the emergency mission in Sierra Leone, he'd viewed it as the perfect escape. Yet he'd come home and placed himself right back in the same situation, hadn't he? What kind of sweet torture was he subjecting himself to this time around? And what kind of firestorm would he set off within his family, he wondered, if he acted on his feeling for Ava?

Ava stood on the dunes with her arms wrapped around her middle, the wind whipping through her hair as the sun warmed her cheeks. From this distance she could watch the twins on the beach without being too overbearing. She had to constantly resist the urge to smother them with her love, to wrap them up in a little protective cocoon where nothing or no one could ever hurt them. They were so tiny and vulnerable. It made her heart ache just to watch them.

But she knew she had to let go, at least a little bit. Casey and Dolly were already balking at her overprotective nature, and they weren't even seven years old yet. It was only a matter of time before it all blew up in her face. She didn't need a child psychologist to tell her what happened to kids who were treated like fragile pieces of china. So, after praying on it for the past few weeks, she was taking matters into her own hands and trying to give them a little more independence.

Ten minutes ago she'd picked up the kids from school and headed straight over to Sandy Neck Beach. Sawyer had called this morning and invited them to watch his team conduct rescue maneuvers on the ocean. The kids had been ecstatic. Ever since they'd seen him the other night, Casey had been peppering her with nonstop questions about when he could see Uncle Sawyer again. He was clearly itching to visit him at his lighthouse. And she'd overheard the twins whispering about asking Sawyer to go to a father-child event at the park. Being invited to watch him in his element was a treat for the twins. Although a panicky feeling bubbled up inside her at the idea of water rescues, she was trying to tamp down her fears so the twins could freely enjoy themselves. She had to remind herself constantly that they weren't in any danger.

At the moment Casey and Dolly were knee-deep in the water watching as rescue swimmers were being dropped into the water from helicopters two hundred or so feet away from the beach. As far as she could tell, they were simulating a rescue scenario in the rough surf. She didn't envy them. Just watching them from this distance made her shiver. The water was choppy and rough, not to mention freezing cold. After twenty minutes or so, she began to walk down to the water's edge where the twins were watching the rescue in progress, their mouths agape as one of the rescuers dangled from a rope and dropped down into the sea. Seeing Sawyer and his team in action was impressive, she realized. After all, it wasn't every day you were able to see heroes in action.

In the distance she could see one of the team swimming from the rescue site toward the beach. He was using his arms and upper body strength to rapidly propel himself through the rough waters. She would recognize Sawyer anywhere. He'd always been an exceptional swimmer, ever since they were children. A few summers he'd even been a lifeguard. The kids were pointing at him and making a commotion as he cut a path through the water. Within minutes, Sawyer came striding out of the water, his body encased in a wet suit. As soon as they saw it was him, they swarmed around him, talking over one another in their attempt to get his attention.

"That was so cool," Casey raved, his eyes sparkling with wonder. "You're like a superhero." His little face was full of admiration.

Ava knew Sawyer hated the hero title, but he didn't seem to mind Casey giving him the label, judging from the wide grin on his face. She couldn't help staring as he put an arm around her son. He pulled at Dolly's pigtail and grazed her cheek with the palm of his hand. Dolly made a face and swatted his hand away, shouting out, "Your hands are like ice." Sawyer threw his head back and laughed before turning toward Dolly and holding his hands up in a menacing way. She let out a high-pitched shriek and ran away, only to find Sawyer at her heels. Within seconds Casey had caught up, and Ava felt a little hitch in her heart as she watched her son shadowing Sawyer. Every little boy needed a man in his life to look up to, and Sawyer was rapidly earning that position in her son's world.

In her opinion Sawyer looked every inch the hero, and it had nothing to do with his profession. The way he was with her kids, the gentle, loving manner in which he interacted with them took her breath away. He was so natural. There was nothing practiced or phony about his love and affection for the twins. It made her feel grateful. For so long now she'd been tormented by everything her family had lost. For the first time in a long while she had something to rejoice about. In this moment she wanted to thank God for bringing Sawyer back to them.

Lord, thank You for bringing Sawyer home. Thank You for allowing him to be a presence in my children's lives. They so desperately need a male presence in their world. Thank You for helping me deal with my anger toward Sawyer so my children can still have him in their lives.

"Is that a special helicopter?" Dolly asked, her finger pointed toward the air. Her eyes were like saucers, and for once, she seemed almost speechless.

"Yes, it is, Dolly. It's an HH-60 Jayhawk," Sawyer explained. "We use it for search-and-rescue missions."

"Whoa! That sounds like something out of a movie." Casey sounded awestruck. Like most six-year-old boys, he was all about the bells and whistles. "The kids at school won't even believe it."

A grin tugged at the corners of Sawyer's mouth. "It's very real, I promise. Today we were training some rescue swimmers." He pointed in the direction of the water. "See how rough those surfs are?" When both of the twins nodded, he continued. "We have to be ready at all times to help people who are in trouble and watch over this land we love so much." Sawyer's voice was solemn. The twins were looking at him as if he were made of solid gold.

"Everyone says you're a hero. I know if you'd been there, you could've saved our daddy." Dolly's words were to the point and matter-of-fact. She didn't seem upset or sad. For the first time since Billy's death, Ava realized that her kids were healing. They weren't broken as she'd feared. Their oversized hearts hadn't been crushed by tragedy.

Sawyer reached out and squeezed Dolly's little hand. "I would like to have done that." He let out a huff of air, and she could tell he was struggling to keep it together. Although their relationship hadn't been perfect, Sawyer and Billy had been close friends. Ava knew how deeply Sawyer had grieved when they'd lost him.

There was a story behind the hero label. Back when Sawyer was beginning his career as an officer, he'd been part of a rescue mission during which he'd plucked a family of four out of the raging sea during a nor'easter. The daring rescue had made national headlines. Sawyer had been labeled a hero, a moniker he'd been fighting against ever since. As she gazed at her children, noting the adoration on their faces, she knew Sawyer would always be a hero in their eyes.

"Race you to the lifeguard chair, Dolly." Casey tossed out the challenge and then took off, causing Dolly to loudly object before she raced after him.

"You know you're a rock star, right?" Ava asked as she studied Sawyer's satisfied expression. As excited as the kids were about being able to watch Sawyer and his team, she was equally impressed. To see him in his element was awe-inspiring.

"It's easy being a rock star when I'm not the one making them eat their vegetables and tidy up their rooms." He gazed at her, his eyes shining with admiration. "You're the real hero, Ava. What you and the kids have been through would have torn apart most families." He shook his head. "From what I can see, Casey and Dolly are healthy, happy and well-loved kids. That's all because of you."

Sawyer's words reached down deep and touched a part of her soul. It wasn't easy raising children in the aftermath of tragedy. Most days she worried about their peace of mind and whether they were happy and whole. More than anything she tended to worry about whether they had lasting memories of Billy and if they felt different from other kids who had fathers. Even though she considered herself a bit broken, it was nice to know she'd successfully shouldered her children through the worst storm of their lives and kept them solidly grounded.

"Thanks for saying that. It's nice to know I've kept them on track." She let out a deep sigh and allowed her shoulders to relax. "There were some tough days. The nights seemed endless. Sometimes when I couldn't sleep I would just lie awake and listen to the pounding of my heart. And I used to replay his voice over and over on the answering machine because I knew it was the only way I could hear his voice again. Believe it or not, I still haven't gotten around to cleaning out the last few things in his closet." She sniffled back raw emotion. "Somehow we weathered through it."

"You're a strong woman. You could serve as an inspiration to so many women raising kids by themselves."

She didn't know if she deserved such admiration. When the bottom had fallen out of her world, she knew there were really only two choices—sink or swim. She'd doggy-paddled her way through the mountain of grief, managing to keep her head slightly above water. And she hadn't done it alone. No, there had been soldiers in her camp who'd fought the hard battles right alongside her.

"You had a part in this, Sawyer. I was frozen in the weeks after Billy first died. I'll never forget how you stepped in with the kids. Between you, Billy's parents and my sisters—"

She swallowed past the painful memories, choosing

instead to live in the moment. "I'm fortunate to have so many people who love me."

The wind had kicked up now and it was starting to get a bit gusty. She wondered how Sawyer wasn't freezing in his wet suit. He reached out and brushed a few strands of hair out of her eyes. His eyes locked on hers, and she felt a chill race down her arms.

"You are loved, Ava. So very much," Sawyer murmured, his eyes never breaking contact with her own. He reached out and slid his hand in hers, the same way he'd done so a hundred times or more when they'd raced across this beach as children, screaming at the top of their lungs. But now everything around them was quiet, save for the muted cries of a flock of seagulls and the hushed tones of the twins as they sat in the lifeguard chair. It was nice to have a still moment with Sawyer where no words were needed to fill the silence. With a look or a gesture, they always knew where the other stood. It had always been that way between them, and she prayed it would never change. Sawyer was her cornerstone.

For the first time in a long while she was beginning to feel like her old self, the one who wasn't afraid of losing people she loved and who embraced the world around her. She felt stronger, firm in the knowledge that her children were thriving and centered. Despite everything they'd endured, they were happy. Dolly and Casey were the focus of her life, for now and always. With the grace of God she'd be able to guide them on through childhood into adulthood. She smiled as she imagined the future—first dates, proms, driving lessons, weddings. There was so much to look forward to on the horizon. The only thing causing her worry at the moment was the bubbly feeling in the pit of her stomach whenever she gazed into Sawyer's soulful brown eyes.

Chapter Four

It's a beautiful day for a wedding, Ava thought as she pulled up outside Sea Street Church.

The sun was shining brightly, with the temperature hovering at seventy degrees. The sky was robin's egg–blue and cloudless. The historic church sat on top of a hill overlooking Cape Cod Bay. Renowned for its beautiful stained-glass windows and the pebbled stonework on its facade, Sea Street Church was a historic landmark in Buzzards Bay. It wasn't unusual to see tourists lined up to take pictures in front of the stained-glass windows or the marble statues in the courtyard. There were many days she'd come to Sea Street Church seeking a quiet place to pray. But that was years ago, she realized. Long before she'd reached a stalemate with God.

Her mother-in-law had already picked up the twins and brought them to the church so they could take pictures with the bridal party prior to the ceremony. She could only hope they were on their best behavior. Ava took a deep breath as she prepared to walk up the stone steps and into the church. It had been a while since she'd graced the church with her presence. As she walked inside, she felt a tidal wave of emotion wash over her. This sacred place held a lot of memories, both sweet and shattering. She'd gotten married in this church, Pastor Felix had baptized her children within these walls and she'd bid her parents farewell here, along with her husband. So much loss, and yet today, everyone was gathering here to celebrate the union of two people who wanted to spend the rest of their lives together, who were about to pledge to each other their undying fidelity. It was a joyous event.

Although she loved weddings, a small part of her felt sad that this part of her life was over. Love, romance, marriage. Having someone finish her sentences because they knew her so well. It was all a thing of the past. She couldn't imagine opening up her heart to another person, not when loving Billy and losing him had caused her so much heartache. Loving someone meant running the risk of dealing with unbearable loss. Heartache. Been there, done that. She wasn't going down that road again.

Her head in the clouds, she ran straight into a solid presence as she turned the corner. Strong arms steadied her. She looked up to find warm, blue eyes gazing upon her.

"Pastor Felix!" she cried out, flustered at his sudden appearance. Although she'd braced herself for this encounter, a wave of shame washed over her. It had been ages since she'd attended service. She couldn't imagine what he must think of her.

"I haven't seen you in a long time, Ava. This church isn't the same without you." He leaned forward and pressed a kiss against her cheek.

Ava grimaced. "It's been a while since the kids and I have attended service," she acknowledged. She felt her cheeks getting warm with embarrassment.

Pastor Felix smiled at her, his eyes filled with compassion. "My comment wasn't a judgment. Just my way of saying you've been missed. You and the twins."

"Thank you. Hearing that means a lot to me," she said in a low voice, moved by his words. "I just haven't felt moved to worship."

A puzzled look passed over his face. "Is there a reason you're feeling this way?"

"Let's just say God and I had a little falling-out," she hedged. Now wasn't the time or place to get into a discussion about her fractured relationship with God. She'd come to Sea Street Church this morning to celebrate a wedding, not to air out her past grievances with the Lord.

Pastor Felix nodded. "Because of Billy's passing?" he pressed.

She nodded, tears welling up in her eyes as she admitted the truth she'd been hiding for two long years. "Yes. After I lost him I couldn't help wondering why God didn't answer any of my prayers." It felt good to say the words out loud, to admit her pent-up feelings to Pastor Felix. Whatever she might say to him, she knew he wouldn't view her in a negative light. He was a fair man.

"It's normal to question your faith after such a devastating tragedy. And you've had a lot of loss in your life. Your parents passing so close to each other, then Billy. You've shouldered a lot of grief in a short period of time."

And Sawyer. She had to add him to the list, as well. For a while there, she'd lost him, too. The thought came to her like a bolt out of the blue, and for the first time in years she acknowledged to herself how deeply she'd suffered. Inexplicably, she'd always thought of her losses as separate events, rather than one tidal wave of grief and pain.

"Yes, I've had a lot of loss over the years," she admitted. "The hits just kept coming."

For years she'd been so busy forging through the pain she'd never stopped long enough to grieve all her loved ones. Through it all, she'd tried to be invincible. Too much so, she now realized. She'd never wanted the kids to see the depths of her suffering, her unbearable grief. In the end, it hadn't helped her healing process to bottle everything up inside. She was still in limbo and holding on to things she needed to let go of.

"What can I do to help you?" Pastor Felix's voice enveloped her like a warm breeze.

"I'm not sure." Ava shook her head. "I've missed Sea Street Church. Lately, I've wanted to come back and attend service, but two years is such a long time to have been away. Even today my stomach is full of knots."

"Ava, don't let embarrassment or fear stand in your way," he continued. "One of your most special qualities is the way you connect with others. I'll never forget how you drove Mr. P to church every Sunday without fail when he lost the use of his leg. He leaned on you, and you were there for him. If you lean on this congregation, they'll support you, Ava."

Tears welled in her eyes as she remembered her close bond with Mr. P. Ravaged by diabetes, he'd been unable to drive after his leg was amputated. It had been her pleasure to drive him to Sea Street Church so he could worship and experience fellowship with the rest of the congregation. As well as being a lifelong friend, Mr. P had served as an inspiration. Despite being ill and in pain, he'd continued to be a bright light in the world, spreading cheer wherever he went. He'd almost made it to his ninetieth birthday. It made her ashamed to realize how closed off she'd been in the past few years.

The sound of footsteps had them both pausing in their private conversation. Sawyer appeared in the hallway, looking impossibly handsome in a light-colored linen blazer, a polo shirt and tan Dockers. Ava felt something shift inside her at the sight of him. Her pulse quickened. As soon as he saw them, his eyes lit up with pleasure. He reached their side in a few, easy strides.

"Pastor Felix, how are you?" Sawyer reached his hand out and the two clasped hands.

"I'm well, Sawyer. I've been sending a lot of prayers your way."

"I deeply appreciate that," Sawyer answered. "As far as I'm concerned, prayer is the best gift anyone could ever give me."

"Spoken like a true man of faith," Pastor Felix responded. He rubbed his hands together. "Well, if the two of you will excuse me, I should check in with the bride and groom. The ceremony should be starting in a half hour or so." As he walked by Sawyer he patted him on the shoulder. "I want to hear all about your trip the next time I see you."

"Will do," Sawyer answered with an easy smile. "There's plenty to tell."

After Pastor Felix disappeared down the hall, Sawyer turned all of his attention to her. "You okay?" he asked. His eyes were like laser beams as they skimmed over her face.

"I'm good. We had a nice talk. I was able to get some things off my chest," she answered, her heart feeling lighter than it had in ages. It felt good to be totally open with someone who wouldn't judge or misunderstand her. Pastor Felix had given her food for thought. Later on this evening, in the quiet time after the kids had gone to sleep, she would reflect on Pastor Felix's words.

Sawyer raised an eyebrow. She knew he was champing at the bit to ask her the specifics about their conversation, but his excellent home training wouldn't allow him to pry. Ava decided to take pity on him.

"I've been angry at God for a long time," she explained. "It's something I've been working on for a while. I still haven't been able to fully move past it. Pastor Felix helped me realize I shouldn't try to do it alone. I need this church. And the congregation."

"The folks who make up this congregation are amazing. Do you know they started a special prayer circle for me while I was overseas?" Sawyer's voice was full of admiration and awe. "I can't tell you how much that humbles me."

Ava began fiddling with her fingers. "I'm embarrassed to say I didn't know about it. I've been out of the loop for a while."

"It's nothing to be ashamed about. You're struggling a bit right now with your faith. We've just got to find a way to get you back on track." He leaned toward her, his cheek brushing against hers as he whispered in her ear, "Meet me in the back pew." A woodsy smell filled her nostrils, and she felt the slight roughness of his stubble grazing against her skin. She fought the sudden urge to press a kiss against his cheek.

An image of a ten-year-old Sawyer came rushing back to her. He'd been adorable—with big eyes the color of a Hershey bar, impossibly crooked teeth and brown skin burnished from the sun. Every week they'd attended Sunday school together in the basement of Sea Street Church. When class was finished the children were ushered upstairs to attend Sunday service. Many of the kids rushed to the front of the church in order to sit in the first pew, but the very idea gave Sawyer the willies. As soon as class ended he would whisper in her ear to meet him in the back pew of the church. And each and every time she did, there had been plenty of mischief concocted by Sawyer. "I always got in trouble when I sat with you," she reminded him. She felt her mouth curving upward into a smile. "And you always had to stay after church to speak to the pastor."

"Come on. I wasn't that bad, was I?" His voice sounded incredulous.

Ava burst into giggles. "You were incorrigible. Remember the time you put marbles in the collection basket?"

A huge grin threatened to split his face wide open. "I'll never forget the look on Pastor McIntyre's face when he stood at the pulpit and announced that the weekly collection yielded three hundred dollars and twenty-six marbles."

"And then he looked straight to the back of the church, directly at you."

Memories of a simpler time warmed her heart. Pastor McIntyre had retired years ago, but she still thought of him with fondness. He'd been on the strict side, but he'd taught them all the important things about church, community and loving the Lord.

She eyed Sawyer, a feeling of warmth spreading through her as they took a walk down memory lane. "You were quite the cutup."

"And you were the prettiest girl in Sunday school."

"No," she said with a shake of her head. "That would've been my sister, Sunny. I was the tomboy who wouldn't have been caught dead in a dress. Remember?"

"How could I forget? The first time I ever saw you in a dress, it nearly bowled me over. It was a lavender color with lilacs all over it. You wore purple shoes to match."

"I can't believe you remember that." Her voice was filled with awe. "Mama had to practically tie me down so I would wear it." Just the thought of her sweet, gentle mother caused a longing so deep to bubble up from inside her it made her a bit breathless. Time hadn't changed a thing. She still missed her mother terribly.

The ache had eased a bit, but the yearning was ever present.

"I remember everything, Ava." He reached out and tipped her chin up so their gazes were locked. His stare was intense, and she found herself feeling a bit self-conscious. Even though she'd never had a problem making conversation with Sawyer, she suddenly felt tongue-tied. It didn't make sense her feeling this way, all jittery and nervous. She'd been friends with him for most of her life. Perhaps it was the way his hand lingered on her face, sending chills through her entire body.

Just then the sound of a door banging shut had them both startled and turning toward the front door of the church. Her father-in-law was standing there with a huge scowl on his face, staring directly at the two of them.

Sawyer felt an immediate shift in his own mood as soon as he laid eyes on his uncle. His hand dropped to his side and he moved a step away from Ava. He clenched, then unclenched his fists. Tension hummed in the air as Uncle Troy stood on the threshold, his mouth set in a grim line. Ava had a worried look on her face, making him wonder if she had any idea that her father-in-law had a problem with the two of them appearing as thick as thieves.

"Dad, is everything okay?" Ava asked. "You look upset."

"Everything's fine," he said, the corners of his mouth lifting in the hint of a smile. Sawyer sensed it was just a put on for propriety's sake. Uncle Troy wouldn't ruin the festive vibe by voicing his concerns about their close relationship. In an effort to ease the tension, Sawyer walked toward his uncle, his arms held wide open for a hug. Much like his father, Uncle Troy was tall and wide-shouldered, possessing the build of a football player. Sawyer watched as the corners of his mouth pulled upward into the hint of a smile. Uncle Troy lifted his arms and pulled him into the tightest of bear hugs.

"Sawyer, it's good to see you back where you belong." His tone was laced with emotion. As a former marine, Uncle Troy prided himself on being tough and no-nonsense. Sawyer knew all too well that beneath his gruff exterior lay a tenderhearted soul. He was simply a man who wasn't always comfortable showing affection.

"I'm happy to be back," Sawyer said as they pulled apart from each other. He watched his uncle blink away the moisture in his eyes.

"It's good to see you." Ava placed a kiss on her father-in-law's cheek. "How was your doctor's appointment? Is your blood sugar okay?"

Uncle Troy grimaced. "My blood sugar is fine. Unfortunately, my blood pressure is higher than it should be, courtesy of the five pounds I gained over the holidays." He patted his slight belly. "Other than that, I'm right as rain."

Uncle Troy had been diagnosed as borderline diabetic, so his doctors were constantly advising him to exercise and keep his weight down. Those five pounds would have to come off sooner rather than later.

As more and more people began streaming into the

church, Sawyer glanced at his watch. "We better move inside if we want to get a good seat."

"I should go on back and find the kids. Why don't the two of you go find a seat?" Ava suggested before leaving them to head toward the private rooms. He couldn't resist sneaking a last glance at her as she walked away. The pink dress she was wearing fit her like a dream, showcasing her petite figure, small waist and shapely legs. She looked beautiful, and he felt a pang of regret that he hadn't told her so.

When he turned back around, Uncle Troy was gazing at him, a wary expression etched on his face. He opened his mouth to say something, then quickly closed it. Sawyer had the feeling he was biting his tongue. They both knew it wasn't the time or the place to get into it about his close relationship with Ava. This was the bride and groom's special day, and they deserved to have everyone's attention squarely focused on them.

As he walked down the aisle with his uncle, Sawyer couldn't help noticing the festive adornments inside the church. Every pew was marked with a white satin bow and a sweet scent hovered in the air, courtesy of the massive floral decorations gracing the altar. He glanced to the front of the church where a handsome man with olive skin tugged at his collar as his best man tried to help him adjust his bow tie. Within minutes they were joined in their pew by Daniel and his parents, followed shortly by Ava's sisters, Ella and Sunny, who sat behind them. Daniel was practically floating on air, since he'd been asked to do a reading. He'd kept it a big secret from everyone exactly which passage he'd selected, wanting it to be a surprise.

Right before the ceremony started, Ava darted into the pew in front of him. She was seated at the end of the aisle, a camera clutched in her hand. He had to smile at the air of nervous expectation hovering around her. As much as she loved the twins, he knew she was bursting with pride from their special role in the ceremony. The air inside the church crackled with energy.

This is the day which the Lord hath made, we will rejoice and be glad in it. The psalm came to him, reminding him of all the happiness surrounding him today. The joy was infectious. It vibrated and hummed in the air. Providence had placed him in this very church on this sacred day. But for God's mercy, he might not have made it back home to his loved ones.

As the strains of the "Wedding March" rang out in the church, Dolly made her way down the aisle, solemnly dropping rose petals with every step she took. Casey followed a few feet behind his sister, his pace increasing rapidly as he neared the front of the church. He couldn't help smiling as he watched Ava giving Casey the signal to slow down. As soon as they reached the front of the church, the twins joined their mother in her pew. A sudden hush fell over the congregation as the bride glided down the aisle, supported on both sides by her parents. She was beaming from ear to ear, her smile almost contagious. His aunt Tabby and uncle Frank looked choked up as they handed their daughter off to her groom.

The ceremony was heartfelt and moving. As Daniel

stood at the altar and recited from Song of Solomon, his mother teared up and dabbed at her eyes with a tissue. "Many waters cannot quench love, neither can floods drown it." Daniel's voice rang out strong and sure. Sawyer felt a pang as the words resonated within him. He knew that sentiment all too well. Even if you tried to extinguish it, true love endured.

When Daniel returned to his seat, Ava turned around and gave him a thumbs-up and an endearing smile. He couldn't seem to get his mind off her. Even the slightest movement on her part drew his attention. Sitting behind her, he couldn't help noticing the graceful slope of her neck and the nervous habit she had of raking her fingers through her glossy hair.

The last wedding he'd attended in this church had been Ava and Billy's. The only things he remembered about that ceremony was the awful feeling in the pit of his stomach and the moment when the pastor had declared them man and wife. He'd been fuming and jealous and sickened by his own lack of action. Why hadn't he tried to stop the wedding? Why hadn't he gone to Ava and told her that he loved her, that he'd always loved her? The thought startled him, and he suddenly felt choked by all the emotions of ten years ago. Yes, he'd been in love with her, he acknowledged. But that had been a long time ago, before she married his cousin and built a life with him and their children.

The experience of getting over Ava had brought him to his knees. For months he'd teetered on the edge of destruction, plunging into a depression that had nearly cost him his career. Thankfully, he'd had a commanding officer who'd believed in him and his potential. He sucked in a deep breath as the remembrance of his shattered heart pulled at him. He never wanted to feel that way again. Not in a million years. Because being in love with someone who didn't love you back was a soul-crushing experience, one he had no intention of repeating ever again.

Chapter Five

Ava let out a small cry as a thorn pricked her finger.

She raised her finger to her mouth, blowing on it to get her mind off the pain. Putting the finishing touches on twenty floral centerpieces wasn't easy, especially since they were crunched for time. There was no time to waste if they were going to be ready to receive seventy-five wedding guests at her home within the hour. She had to admit that she missed the challenges and creativity associated with her former job as a party planner. Weeks ago Melanie had asked if she would mind hosting a reception at her house for her and Doug, to be followed by a clambake on the beach. Although that entailed a lot of work, there was no way she could have refused. Billy wouldn't have wanted it any other way. Melanie had been as close to him as a sister. After the ceremony had ended, she'd hightailed it out of the church with the twins in tow and headed home. Her sisters had arrived a few minutes later, both of them eager to help out.

With the help of Sunny and Ella, all of the finishing touches were completed, with the exception of the floral arrangements. Because of a mix-up with the florist, most of the flowers hadn't arrived until this morning. At the moment she and Sunny were creating small centerpieces composed of pink roses, stargazer lilies, white calla lilies and baby's breath. They'd selected all of Melanie's favorite flowers and put them together in a breathtakingly beautiful glass bowl. Although they were nearly done, they still had two more to finish up.

"He is drop-dead gorgeous." Her sister Sunny's voice broke her concentration, causing a sliver of irritation to creep along her spine. This was typical Sunny. Rather than focus on the flowers, she was checking someone out.

"Who are you talking about?" Ava asked, not bothering to look up from her floral arrangement. She wanted to place all the arrangements on the tables before she checked in with the caterer. Pretty soon the guests would start streaming in. This was not the time or the place to listen to her sister rhapsodize about a good-looking guy.

"Who am I talking about?" Sunny threw the question back at her. "Sawyer, that's who. He's one good-looking guy. But I'm sure you've already noticed, what with the history the two of you share."

At the mention of Sawyer's name, she swiveled her head toward the direction of her sister's gaze. Sawyer was standing next to the jazz band as they were setting up, making conversation and looking just as handsome as Sunny had reported. She'd been too busy to even notice his arrival.

Ava shifted her gaze to Sunny, looking at her with a raised eyebrow. She had no idea what her sister was talking about. "Our history? As best friends?"

"Stop being coy, Ava. When we were kids, you and Sawyer were inseparable," Sunny said. "You two were crazy about each other."

Ava felt her cheeks getting flushed. "We were friends, Sunny. That's it!" she insisted.

"Friendship?" Sunny asked with a tilt of her head. "So, back in the day the two of you never held hands or kissed behind the bleachers?"

Kissing Sawyer. The very mention of it brought back a bittersweet memory of her very first kiss. She and Sawyer had been in eighth grade. They'd been best friends for years, ever since Sawyer's family had moved into the house two doors down. They'd been playing at the old quarry, skipping stones over the surface of the water and arguing about the Red Sox and the Yankees. She'd fallen and skinned her knee, tears coursing down her face as she tried her hardest not to sob from the pain. Sawyer had pulled out a bandanna from his pocket, using it to deftly dab at her bloody knee. Once her tears had stopped he'd leaned toward her and planted a sweet, comforting kiss on her lips. Although she'd been clueless about kissing, it had been a pleasant experience. She couldn't imagine a better first kiss than the one she'd shared with Sawyer.

And, of course, she couldn't help reminiscing about that impromptu kiss last summer. Although it had been unexpected, it had been full of comfort and joy, as well as tenderness. For the first time in a long while she'd felt like a woman again. But then she'd been plagued with guilt about betraying her husband's memory, while Sawyer had unceremoniously left the country.

Her sister's comments about Sawyer did something funny to her insides. As far back as she could remember, there was something about her feelings for him that troubled her. For years she'd managed to stuff them so far down inside herself it was easy to pretend they didn't exist. Her loyalty to Billy hadn't even allowed her to examine what those feelings were. She'd been a faithful wife to her husband and she'd never so much as looked at another man. Yet there had always been something about Sawyer that tugged at her. And even though she'd tried to disguise it in a hundred different ways, Billy had known. He'd always known.

"Don't listen to her," her sister Ella advised as she walked past carrying a tray of beautiful cupcakes she would soon transform into a tower. "She's never been able to have a solid friendship with a man without turning it into a romance."

Sunny let out a huff of air. "Well, at least I still believe in romance. You haven't been on a date since the Dark Ages." Ella laughed and playfully swatted her sister. "And you," Sunny said with a pointed look in Ava's direction, "need to get out there and meet new people."

"I'm not ready to…meet people," Ava snapped. "It's only been two years. I'm still trying to make sense of Billy's death. I'm still trying to get my family back to normal."

Sunny and Ella shared a look. From where Ava was standing it appeared to be full of hidden meaning. She knew all too well that her sisters were worried about her and had been for a very long time. The three sisters were as different as the seasons. Sunny was spontaneous and spirited while Ella was friendly and an all-around sweetheart. Ava was the creative, levelheaded one of the bunch—practical, solid. The anchor was what they called her, or at least they had until Billy's passing. In the past two years it felt as if she'd been doing all the leaning on her family. She'd felt incredibly fragile.

Sunny worked as a weather girl at a local television channel on the island. With her statuesque figure, golden-brown complexion and striking features, she was the showstopper. And she knew it! For as long as Ava could remember, her sister had dreamed of leaving Cape Cod and heading off to Hollywood to become a famous movie actress. Ella was beautiful in her own right, but she didn't have the confidence to shine like her sister. With her chocolate-brown skin and curvy figure, she was coming into her own after a long bout with Epstein-Barr virus. She'd recently opened her own healthy bakery, Deliteful, on Ocean Street in town.

"It's not healthy to keep blaming yourself for Billy's death," Ella said. Her big brown eyes teared up. "What happened to him was a tragic accident."

"Billy made a decision to go out on the water that night, even though he'd been—" Sunny stopped short, catching herself before she finished her sentence. Again, her sisters locked glances.

"Drinking? Is that what you were going to say?" Ava

whispered, her throat clogged with emotion. "You don't have to sugarcoat it."

Sunny bit her lip. "Yes, that's what I was going to say." She let out a sigh. "Ava, we keep dancing around things with you because we don't want to hurt you. What you've been through in the past few years has been agonizing. All three of us lost our parents, but you lost so much more. Losing Billy…it was so sudden and shocking." Sunny shook her head in disbelief. "But hiding yourself away at your house, not going to church, avoiding all your friends…it's very worrisome."

"I'm not hiding," she protested. "I've just been trying to simplify things so I could create some normalcy for the kids."

Ella raised an eyebrow. "So how is staying away from Sea Street Church creating normalcy?"

Ava felt her cheeks burn. As far as she was concerned, her relationship with God was a personal matter. It was between her and the big guy upstairs. She didn't owe her sisters an explanation. Some things were truly off-limits, even with family members.

"I don't have to go to church to have a relationship with God," she argued.

"That's true," Ella said in a doubtful voice. "But Ava, you've always loved attending service. You were always the most devout among the three of us."

"It just seems that you've withdrawn a lot since you lost Billy," Sunny added, her eyes wide with concern. "And you've been having those panic attacks. We're just worried about you. We love you."

Ava felt moisture gathering in her eyes and she tried

her best to stop the flow of tears. She loved her sisters more than anything in the world, but she didn't want them worrying about her. As the oldest sister, she had always had the responsibility to hold things together. When their parents had died of cancer within months of each other, she'd been the strong one. She wasn't used to being the one leaning on everyone else for comfort. There was a great deal of shame she felt about her panic attacks. They came out of the blue, without warning, leaving her struggling to breathe and feeling helpless. She'd had her first one a week after Billy died when she was in deep mourning. She'd always thought there was something wrong with the stages of grief. For her, the first stage had been bargaining, followed by denial, anger and depression. Ever since then she'd been stuck—sometimes it felt as if she were miles and miles away from the final stage. Acceptance.

"There's no need to worry. What you don't understand is that grief is a process. I can't just snap my fingers and get over his death. It doesn't work like that."

Ella quickly moved toward her and enveloped her in a hug. "We don't expect you to stop grieving or stop loving him. We just wish you weren't cutting yourself off from so many things you used to love."

Sunny came over and squeezed her hand. "And we know there was a lot of tension between you and Billy before his death. After he lost his job, things were really tough between the two of you."

Ava felt a burst of anger toward her sister. She didn't need to be reminded of all the tough times she and Billy had endured. What purpose did it serve? Her husband was dead and buried. She didn't need Sunny analyzing their marriage problems. What did her single sister know about love and marriage anyway?

"And? Just because we had problems doesn't mean I loved him any less," she snapped.

"That wasn't what I meant—" Sunny began, a look of distress etched on her face.

"He was all I'd ever known. Since I was eighteen years old. Ava and Billy. Cape Cod sweethearts. Of course it wasn't perfect, you guys. We had problems. Serious problems. Things were shaky—he was drinking again and spending too much on things we didn't need. It was like he had this big hole inside him he needed to fill up. And he tried to fill it up with me and the kids, then the house on the beach, then the alcohol. But it wasn't enough. It was never enough."

Her body was trembling, and she could feel hot tears on her cheeks. "And I couldn't get him to go to rehab. I tried so many times, but he always refused. He didn't think he had a drinking problem. And even though I knew he did, I didn't push it. I suppose some people might call that denial. But I was so afraid of everything falling apart that I let it go. And for some reason that I still haven't figured out, Billy went out on the water that night, when he was barely in any condition to walk, never mind navigate the open waters."

"Some things you might never find answers for, Ava. It'll drive you crazy trying to wrap it all up with a nice little bow." Instead of comforting her, Ella's words only served to frustrate her. What if finding answers was the only way of getting closure? What if being at peace with her husband's death continued to elude her?

Sawyer was suddenly standing next to her, his face a mask of concern as his gaze raked over her face. "What's wrong? Why are you crying?" He looked over at Ella and Sunny, his forbidding expression demanding an explanation. He was practically glaring at her sisters.

"It's nothing," she quickly answered as she swiped the tears away. "I always get emotional at weddings."

Sawyer's mouth was set in a firm line. "I think you should take a break before the bride and groom arrive." He quickly glanced at his watch. "They won't be here for another thirty minutes or so. Come on. Let's go."

She let out a nervous laugh. "A break? I don't have time for one. I still have floral arrangements to finish."

"I'll finish them up," Sunny volunteered with a wide grin. Ava knew her sister well enough to know she was smirking. If she took a break with Sawyer, it would just reinforce her sister's belief that there was something more to their relationship than an enduring friendship. Sunny made a shooing gesture with her hands. "Go on. Take a break. Ella and I can handle it."

Before she knew what was happening, she felt Sawyer tightly grip her hand and lead her away from the patio, down toward the path overlooking the beach. He didn't let go of her hand until they'd reached the sand at the bottom of the steps.

She stole a glance at him through lowered lids. He was staring off into the distance, his eyes locked on the tumultuous blue ocean stretching out before him for miles and miles. Once they'd reached the beach he rolled up his sleeves and pant legs, giving him a more casual, relaxed vibe.

"This beach has a lot of memories," he said in a wistful voice. "Treasure hunts by the light of the moon are my all-time favorite ones."

"Mine, too," she said with a sigh. "Is it just me, or was life a whole lot simpler back then?"

He let out an easy laugh. "We were kids. What did we know?"

She looked over at him, buoyed by his gentle spirit. His easy charm never failed to make her feel at ease. "I think we knew a lot. We knew right from wrong. We went to church every Sunday. We respected our elders. And nothing was better than spending time at the beach, whether it was going crabbing or swimming out past the ropes or burying each other in the sand. Everything considered, we were pretty good kids."

She studied Sawyer's profile as he stared out at the water. "Call me crazy," he said, "but there was something pretty wonderful about having to use our imaginations instead of reaching for an electronic device to keep us entertained."

Ava shuddered in an exaggerated way. "The twins aren't there yet. They're still happy playing on the beach and building forts. I hope it stays that way for a while." Her voice sounded wistful to her own ears. If she could, she would slow time down a little so they could stay this age for a bit longer. As it was, it felt as if their lives were going by at warp speed.

As they walked toward the water's edge, Ava dipped her toe in to test the temperature. The water was still frigid despite the warm June temperature. The ocean didn't usually get warm until July, and even then, it had to be at a certain temperature to tempt her to go swimming. She turned back toward her house on the cliff, taking a moment to admire the place she called home. Despite everything, she still loved the fact that her house overlooked the sea. From up there she could gaze upon endless miles of beach and ocean. Even though the sea had stolen Billy away from her, she couldn't leave her cozy house by the water. In the days, weeks and months after her husband's death she'd needed to give Dolly and Casey a sense of stability. Staying in their home by the water had given them a sense of familiarity and comfort.

Every day she'd walked down to the beach and stared out over the water, asking herself how she could love something that had taken so much from her. But the sea called to her. It was beautiful and temperamental. Peaceful, yet churning with emotion. Its timeless rhythms called to her. It owned a piece of her heart. It reminded her of childhood and her parents and collecting seashells with her sisters along Sandy Neck Beach. Forever and always, tangy sea water would flow through her veins.

"You made a fine pirate, Ava Trask."

With those simple words, Sawyer transported her all the way back to childhood. She chuckled as an image of the two of them dressed up as pirates flashed through her mind. They'd hunted for treasure on the beach, courtesy of Mr. P, who'd buried all kinds of booty for them to find. Gold painted coins. Costume jewelry. Swords.

Peacock feathers. He'd gone to great lengths to entertain them.

"Right back at you. If I remember correctly, you really got into character. You had the whole British accent thing going, didn't you?"

Sawyer's eyes crinkled as he laughed. "I wasn't the only one who was into it. You were the prettiest pirate to ever wear an eye patch and wield a sword."

Ava giggled. "We were quite a pair, weren't we?"

"Best friends," Sawyer said, his face taking on a somber quality as he gazed at her.

They had been best friends, until she'd married Billy. Her husband had been too threatened by her friendship with his cousin to allow the relationship to continue. And over a period of weeks, months and years, her relationship with Sawyer had grown weaker. Although they'd still seen each other on occasion, the bond between them diminished over time. And she had allowed it to happen.

"I missed you," Sawyer said. His words didn't need any explanation. They'd always had a language of their own, a special understanding that no one or nothing could breach. He'd just uttered the very words she'd been thinking. This past year without him had been almost unbearable.

"I missed you, too." She looked away from him, suddenly afraid of the intense look in his eyes and the way it made her feel. Her stomach was beginning to feel as if a hundred butterflies were swirling around inside. Although part of her wanted to run from it, another part of her wanted to celebrate the raw feelings he evoked.

It had been so long since she'd felt anything quite so powerful. "I'm feeling a little ashamed that I didn't push harder for our friendship after I married Billy," she admitted. "I should have been stronger."

Sawyer shot her a knowing look. "It would've driven Billy over the edge."

"It might have," she acknowledged. "Or he may have just had to deal with it, to understand the ties that have always bound us together."

After her marriage to Billy, Sawyer and Billy had continued to be close, but her husband had frowned upon her closeness to his cousin. "It just doesn't look right," he'd always said. Out of guilt and a desire to save her marriage, she'd pulled away from Sawyer. And doing so had wounded her terribly. She'd never wanted to consider what it had done to Sawyer.

"I shouldn't have had to choose," she whispered, her head bowed. "It wasn't fair."

He reached out and lifted her chin up with his hand. "You did what was right for your family. On the day you got married, you and Billy became one flesh. I understood that he and the twins came first before anything or anyone else."

"There were times you seemed almost mad at me," she said. "Were you?" She looked at him, curious to hear his answer.

"I could never be mad at you, Ava." He reached out and caressed her cheek. "I was mad at myself for not speaking up before I went off to the Coast Guard Academy. By the time I came back, you and Billy were engaged."

"Speaking up about what?" she asked. Her throat felt dry. She could barely push the words out of her mouth. What would Sawyer have spoken up about? Feelings she'd never suspected he was holding on to?

He smiled at her, a tender smile that went straight to her heart. "It's all water under the bridge. What really matters is that I'll always be here for you. No matter what." He reached for her hand, giving it a little squeeze before letting it go. Something flickered in his eyes. She couldn't be sure, but it looked a little like regret.

The sound of high-pitched screams had them both turning toward the beach. Casey and Dolly were running toward them from the path at breakneck speed, their little legs pumping through the sand. Dolly stumbled and landed on her knees but quickly picked herself up and kept going.

"Uncle Sawyer. Can you toss the ball with us?" Casey asked, his voice sounding slightly winded. Dolly held out a small rubber ball and she was grinning so wide at Sawyer that Ava thought her daughter's teeth might break. Her kids sure knew how to pile on the charm when they wanted something.

"Of course I can play." His eyes had a mischievous glint. "Why don't we ask your mom to join us?"

She held up her hands and took a step backward. "Sorry, guys. I have to go up and help out before the bride and groom arrives." She took a quick look at her watch. "Their session with the photographer should be ending soon. I have to make sure all the tables look pretty." She held up a warning finger at the twins. "I don't want to see any stains on either one of you. We still have a reception to get through."

"We can still change before the clambake, right, Mama?" Casey asked.

She reached down and squeezed his cheek, earning herself a loud groan from her son. She didn't know when it had happened, but her kids were growing up faster than she would like. As of late, Casey tended to resist cheek pinches and Mom kisses. At least Dolly was still good with them, she thought with a sigh.

"You can change into whatever you like for the clambake. By then you'll have had your picture taken with Melanie and Doug, so you'll be good."

"Yes!" Casey shouted in triumph as he raised his arm in the air.

"Let's go play before our time runs out," Sawyer said with a clap of his hands. He ran a few feet down the beach with the twins racing at his heels. She stared after Sawyer and the kids, surprised by the rapid beating of her heart and the moistness of her palms.

Being alone with Sawyer had brought her back to the carefree days of her youth. Being near him made her feel more alive than she'd felt in years. His presence stirred up feelings she wasn't certain she knew how to handle. Despite her best attempts to maintain a platonic relationship with him, it seemed as if her heart had a mind of its own. And it was leading her straight to Sawyer.

Chapter Six

Sawyer didn't think he'd ever seen a happier couple in his life than his cousin and her new husband. The reception was in full swing, brought to life by a joyful bride and groom, Ava's warm hospitality and a lively jazz band. All of Ava's hard work had paid off, given the festive vibe in the air and the laughing, smiling faces of the guests. He was standing off to the side, watching Ava dance with the twins. Dolly was doing the mashed potato while Casey was waving his hands in the air and jumping up and down.

"Why don't you go join them?" His best friend, Colby, had snuck up on him when he wasn't paying attention. He'd been too preoccupied by the sight of Ava, Casey and Dolly cutting a rug to notice his approach. At six foot four and a head of copper-colored hair, Colby wasn't often unobtrusive. He looked at him pointedly. "You know you want to."

Sawyer shook his head. "Nah. It looks like they're having a family moment."

Colby frowned at him, his blue eyes darkening. "Aren't you family?"

"Give it a rest, Colby." He had the feeling Colby was seconds away from getting on his soapbox. His best friend was one of the few people who knew about his feelings for Ava. They'd attended the Coast Guard Academy together and had shared a tight bond ever since. It was Sawyer who'd invited Colby to move to Cape Cod from Washington State after they'd graduated. Although he'd assured him on many occasions that he was no longer in love with Ava, Colby wasn't convinced. He believed that Sawyer was still smitten with the one who got away.

Colby jerked his head in the direction of Ava and the twins. "Go ahead. Live a little."

Live a little. It was an inside joke between the two of them that went all the way back to the academy. Any time either one of them wanted the other to do something, he would utter those three little words. Knowing he wouldn't get any peace until he acquiesced, Sawyer made his way onto the patio turned dance floor. When he reached Ava and the kids, he bent down so he was on eye level with Dolly. "May I have the pleasure of this dance, Dahlia?" He held out his hand and bowed his head as if she were a royal princess.

Dolly looked up at him shyly, her hazel eyes glistening with excitement. She giggled, then covered her mouth with her hand. She then grabbed hold of his hand, allowing him to twirl her around in circles. Not to be outdone, Casey reached for his mother's hand and began spinning her around. He glanced over at Ava. She had her head thrown back, and the sound of her tinkling laughter sounded more beautiful than the live music. She was happy. He didn't know if it was the wedding or the music or dancing with Casey that was making her so happy. And he didn't care, either.

He was just so grateful that Ava was living in the moment and experiencing something wonderful.

He was thankful for this near-perfect day. There had been moments in Sierra Leone when he'd doubted whether his life would be spared. Clearly, God wasn't done with him yet. He still had miles to go on his journey. Being back in the fold of his close-knit family was wonderful. Being able to spend quality time with Casey and Dolly was icing on the cake. And Ava. Mere words couldn't express his gratitude that she'd squashed her anger and forgiven him. Not being part of her life didn't feel like an option.

A tight knot formed in his stomach as a feeling of anxiety settled over him. Things were too perfect. Perhaps it was the calm before the storm. He couldn't help worrying that when Ava learned about his argument with Billy, she'd find it impossible to forgive him. He could try his best to explain, but knowing her blind loyalty to her husband, she'd never want to talk to him again.

Blame. Sometimes when things got real quiet, he thought about his role in his cousin's death. More times than not, as of late, he found it harder to blame himself. Memories of Billy's drunken escapades—the DUI during his last year of college, his refusal to do a stint at rehab, his habit of always having a drink at social events—all pointed toward an underlying issue his cousin had never fully addressed. Sawyer had had this fog hovering over him for the past few years because of the trauma of losing his cousin. The grief within his family had been unspeakable. Coming home to Cape Cod had served as a healing balm. He was looking at things in his life with a new perspective. His experiences in Africa had allowed him to come back to Buzzards Bay with a fresh set of eyes. At some point, when he wasn't paying attention, the fog had lifted.

And although he knew sooner or later he would have to come clean with Ava, he still held a kernel of hope that the truth would shine brightly rather than casting a dark shadow over their lives.

As the beautiful blue skies turned to pewter, the temperature began to dip into the fifties. While the guests headed down the path to the clambake, Ava switched up to more comfortable clothes—a pair of jeans, a short-sleeved shirt and an oversized sweatshirt. Dolly and Casey had already changed into their playclothes and ran ahead of her down to the beach. By the time she made her way down, everyone was standing around the cooking pit as chef Bob from the Lobster Boat began dishing out the food. Within seconds of her bare feet touching the sand, the happy couple made a beeline toward her.

Melanie reached out to embrace her, planting a warm kiss on her cheek. "Ava, Doug and I wanted to thank you for this lovely reception. It means the world to us."

Melanie was grinning from ear to ear, looking radiant in white linen pants and a matching top.

"You're very welcome. It was my pleasure." Although she didn't want to dampen Melanie's spirits, she needed to make mention of Billy on this sacred day. He'd been such a big part of the Trask family and she knew everyone was feeling his absence today. She turned toward Melanie. "You know Billy would have been over the moon about you finding the love of your life. He would be so proud of you today."

Melanie's eyes filled with moisture, and she blinked the tears away. "I miss him so much, Ava. He used to tell me all the time that I was going to find love when I least expected it." She let out a chuckle. "And he was right. Who knew I would find my other half on a fishing outing?"

Ava laughed. "The Lord works in mysterious ways, doesn't He?"

"Melanie told me that you used to do this for a living, Ava," Doug said. He looked around at the tiki torches, the raging bonfire and the blankets scattered on the sand, his face filled with admiration. "If you don't mind my saying so, I think it would be a shame if you didn't get back to work real soon. You're very talented."

"Thank you, Doug. It makes me feel good knowing I've helped to make this day special," she murmured, feeling pleased by the effusive praise. It had been a long time since she'd received a compliment on her party-planning skills. She made a shooing motion with her hands. "Go on and enjoy the clambake, you two. These memories will last you a lifetime."

As they walked away hand in hand with blissful smiles etched on their faces, a million thoughts were racing through her mind. Working on this event had been challenging and invigorating. It made her realize how much she missed her party-planning business. After Billy's death she hadn't possessed the creativity or the wherewithal to continue working with clients. She'd been too busy trying to hold herself together and make sure the twins were happy and healthy. For the past two years they'd been living on the money she'd received from Billy's life insurance policy. But that money wouldn't last forever. It was a sobering thought. With a mortgage to pay, two children to feed and clothe, plus incidentals, she needed a steady income. Next year the twins would be in first grade, which meant they would be in school full-time. Pretty soon she'd have a lot of time on her hands to dedicate herself to building her business back up.

It was a little scary knowing that her family's financial future rested on her shoulders.

"Penny for your thoughts. You look as if you're trying to figure out how to accomplish world peace." Sawyer walked up, juggling two plates in his hands laden with food. Lobster tails. Baked beans. Corn on the cob. Clams. Shrimp. Ribs. It seemed as if he'd taken a sampling of everything.

"Sure you can handle all that?" she asked with a grin. Her stomach growled as the scent of the food wafted in her direction, reminding her that she'd barely eaten anything all day. She hadn't realized how hungry she was until this very moment.

"This one's for you," he said, offering her a plate while holding the other one steady. "You've worked really hard today. It's time you took a load off your feet." He nodded in the direction of one of the Adirondack chairs they'd set up near the cooking pit. Ava settled into the chair, letting out a contented sigh as her tired feet finally got a break. He quickly pulled another chair over and lowered himself into it.

Sawyer's considerate gesture warmed her heart. Being thoughtful was his sweet spot. It was one of the qualities she found most endearing about him. When she was knee-deep in mourning he'd come to her rescue, doing things for her that she'd never be able to repay him for. He'd cooked for her, done her grocery shopping, taken her to doctor appointments and planned countless outings for Casey and Dolly. He'd offered her a lifeline when she'd been sinking, and she'd held on to it for dear life.

The truth was she'd had this weight on her chest ever since Billy died. Sometimes it felt as if it might pull her under. And now, because of Sawyer, the tight feeling was beginning to loosen up. She'd experienced more happiness today than in the past year combined. The wedding had served as a reminder of life's beautiful moments, while Sawyer's soothing presence had lifted her up.

As she watched Doug take Melanie in his arms and guide her across the sand to the rhythms of the jazz band, she felt a strong sense of community. For so long now she'd avoided social gatherings. Looking around her, she recognized old family friends, parishioners from Sea Street Church and a handful of classmates from high school. Sunny and Ella were being sociable and talking with a group of friends. The twins were running along the water's edge with Daniel. Her in-laws were holding hands and swaying side to side to the music. It was nice to see the two of them so relaxed and upbeat. Losing their only child had been a devastating blow, one they were still struggling to recover from.

Beside her, she felt the full impact of Sawyer's strong, powerful presence. Charming, wonderful Sawyer. His arm brushed against hers, and she felt a shiver of awareness run through her. He was so solid, so incredibly masculine and reliable. She would trust him with her life and those of her children. His nearness was making her think thoughts she'd assumed were dead and buried.

After Billy, she couldn't imagine ever wanting to be with another man, to press her lips against anyone other than her husband. Now her mind wandered back to a certain soul-stirring kiss with Sawyer that had nothing to do with friendship. Even though the kiss was a year old, she remembered it vividly. It had started out as comfort, then quickly blossomed into something powerful. They'd both been stunned into silence afterward, neither one of them knowing what to say or do to get things back to normal.

Right now she just wanted to lay her head on his chest or reach out and clasp her hand with his. Anything, just to be connected with him. The urge to reach out and touch him was making her fingers feel restless.

Jolted by where her thoughts had taken her, she placed her free hand in her lap where it could do no damage. What was she thinking anyway? She needed to be realistic about the situation. The last time she'd shared an intimate moment with Sawyer, it had led to his abrupt departure from Cape Cod. If she was being honest with herself, she'd admit that forgiving Sawyer was still a work in progress. Although they were in a good place, there were still moments when she worried about him leaving again and what it would do to the twins. And her. What would it do to her if she didn't have him in her everyday life? She couldn't deny she had a huge stake in this. Having already lost Sawyer once, she wasn't about to run the risk of losing him a second time.

As the reception wound down, guests began to wander off into the night, all of them heaping praise on Ava as they departed. Sawyer could see the pride on her face, filled with the knowledge that she'd executed a memorable and lively event. The twins were curled up on a blanket, half-asleep and rubbing their eyes. He gently hoisted Casey up in his arms, followed by Dolly. He felt a little hitch in his heart as Dolly curled up against his chest, her little head resting on his shoulder. Casey let out a contented sigh that made its way straight to his heart.

"I wish I could pretend I didn't need your help with that, but I haven't been able to lift them since they were four." Ava reached out and smoothed back Dolly's hair. The look on her face was filled with so much love he felt privileged to witness it.

"It's been a long day for them. Are you ready to head up to the house?"

Ava nodded, grabbing a handful of tiki torches as she said good-night to the band, who had just about packed up their equipment. He started walking up the path, making sure he had a firm grip on both of the kids as he picked up his pace. When they were a few feet away from the house, Ava walked ahead of him and opened up the back door. She flipped a switch, turning on a lamp that cast a subtle glow over the downstairs hallway. Sawyer made his way upstairs, closely followed by Ava. He reached Dolly's bedroom first. Her pink, frilly room was every little girl's dream, bursting with stuffed animals, books and dolls. Ava pulled down the covers, and he laid her in the bed, watching as she turned on her side and curled up in a fetal position. He reached down and grazed his palm against her cheek as something warm inside him bubbled up to the surface. As he turned away he saw Ava lean down to give Dolly a good-night kiss. He heard her whisper, "This day is done, my little one. May God keep you until the morning sun."

The bedtime prayer moved him. He hadn't heard it spoken since he was a child when his own mother would recite it to him as he drifted off to sleep. Despite Ava's fears that she'd strayed away from her spirituality, her actions spoke volumes. She wasn't as far off course as she thought. The Lord was still ever present in her world, even though she was still searching for a way to reconnect with her faith. As Casey rustled in his arms, he made his way through the doorway connecting their adjoining rooms. He heard Ava's soft footsteps behind him as he placed Casey down on the bed.

"Good night, sweet prince," she murmured as she pulled the covers up over him and pressed a kiss against his forehead. "May the Lord keep you in the palm of His hand." As the light went out, a dozen or so fluorescent stars lit up the ceiling, casting a celestial glow to the room.

A memory, sharp and sweet, swept over him. It came to him so clearly, as if it were being shown on a television screen rather than in his mind's eye. As a kid, Ava had been a big fan of astronomy. Matter of fact, for the longest time she'd planned on becoming an astronomer. On the occasion of a summer meteor shower, Mr. P had invited them, along with a few other guests, to watch the monumental occasion from the parapet of his lighthouse. They'd been sitting outside, blanketed in the blackest of nights, shivering in the winter's chill.

"Look, Sawyer. Over there by the Big Dipper!" Ava had shouted, tugging him by the arm and looking up toward the heavens.

"Where? I don't see anything," he'd said in an impatient voice, eager to experience the meteor shower. He'd hated the idea of missing out on something.

"Over there." She'd pointed up toward the velvet sky. "By the handle." No telescope had been necessary. The shooting star exploded in the obsidian sky like a ball of fire. Reds and oranges lit up the night sky. Seeing Ava's face as they saw one shooting star after another—wide eyes, a radiant expression, pure wonder—was something he would never forget. To this day he still didn't know what had affected him more—the meteor shower or the sight of an awestruck Ava.

As he said good-night to Ava and made his way across the sand to his lighthouse, his heart was filled to the brim with his blessings. Thanks to the Lord's gracious gifts, he was back in Buzzards Bay with his family and friends.

Today, he'd been surrounded by so much love. It had vibrated and hummed in the very air around him. Inspired by the joyous union of Melanie and Doug, he couldn't help yearning for something of his own. A soft place to fall. A peaceful refuge from the storms of life. Kids to tuck in at night when the day was done. Someone to belong to, not just for a little while, but for all time.

What he wanted more than anything was love. Pure, wondrous, knock-him-off-his-feet love. He wanted to walk down the aisle with the woman of his dreams and pledge his everlasting love and fidelity to her. He wanted children…lots and lots of them. He wanted someone to stand beside and take care of when the seas became rough. Going through life alone no longer held any appeal. And when he imagined it all unfolding—the courtship, the wedding, the happily ever after—it was always Ava's stunning face that came into sharp focus.

Chapter Seven

Sawyer was up to his knees in sand. Daniel was on all fours, digging a massive moat for his sand castle. Although he'd tried to get his brother to scale the project down, Daniel had insisted on going big. Trying to reason with him was like telling the sun not to shine. When he was in one of his creative moods it just wasn't possible. So here he was, on his day off, no less, helping his brother craft a replica of Versailles, the famous French castle. As a history buff, Daniel wanted to pay homage to a place he dreamed of one day visiting.

Sawyer had to admit he was having a blast. Spending time with Daniel was a luxury he hadn't been afforded for an entire year. Filled with boundless energy, creativity and a genuinely good heart, his brother made even the mundane things in life seem like an adventure.

They'd walked a mile down the beach from his lighthouse to get to this section of beach, passing by Ava's house on the way. He'd been tempted to drop by to check in on her and the kids, but he'd stopped himself, not wanting to wear out his welcome. The last thing he wanted to be was a nuisance.

It had been a week since he'd spent time with them—largely owing to the long hours he'd logged at the Cape Cod Air Station—and he keenly felt their absence. Friday had been their last day of school, and the twins were now officially on summer vacation. The last time he'd spoken with Ava, she had been looking at summer camp options, vacillating between a half-day camp in town and having them home for the summer. For selfish reasons he hoped Ava opted not to enroll them at Camp Tidewater. That way he'd be able to plan adventures with them on his off days.

He cast his gaze upward, studying Ava's house on the bluff. With its light blue shutters and white facade, the house was a modernized version of a classic Cape Cod cottage. A few years ago, the house had been renovated, with a second story being added to the structure. Perched on the cliff overlooking the ocean, it was one of the most visually stunning homes in town. Even from this distance, Sawyer could feel the strong sense of home and hearth emanating from the Trask home.

"Can we go visit Casey and Dolly?" Daniel asked, his eyes now trained on the cottage.

"I'm not sure if they're home today," he hedged. He felt badly as he watched Daniel's face crumple in disappointment. Perhaps he should just head up there and see if Ava and the kids were at home. What harm could it do?

"Look!" Daniel shouted, his finger pointed at three

figures walking along the shore from the other direction. "It's them! Ava, Casey and Dolly."

As they came closer, Sawyer realized Daniel was right. Casey and Dolly must have spotted them also, since they began running toward them, their little legs pumping in the sand. Ava was walking behind them at a leisurely pace, stopping every now and then to pick up a seashell and place it in the bucket she held. She raised a hand and waved to them.

"What are you guys building?" Casey asked as soon as he reached them, breathing heavily from exertion.

"We're building a castle," Daniel said, his eyes gleaming with excitement. "Do you want to help us?"

The twins nodded enthusiastically and scrambled over to his side. Daniel handed Dolly a shovel and gave Casey one of his extra buckets. Casey ran down to the water to fill it up just as Ava joined them. She was dressed casually in a pair of blue capri pants and a white cardigan. Her hair was swept up in a short ponytail, and she was barefoot. She placed her pail on the sand and folded her arms across her chest, gazing upon the sand castle with clear admiration in her eyes.

"Guys, this is amazing. I've never seen a sand castle this impressive," she raved.

"Daniel gets all the credit," Sawyer answered with a shake of his head. "He conceived this idea based on pictures he's seen of Versailles. Believe it or not, he did this from memory."

"I'm not good at a lot of things, but I have a really good memory and I'm a good builder," Daniel chimed in. "Someday, I want to be an architect."

A sense of pride gripped Sawyer as he heard his brother's words. Despite Daniel's limitations, he was determined to reach for his dreams. It would break Daniel's heart if he wasn't able to successfully chase the career goal he'd nurtured since childhood. For as long as Sawyer could remember, his brother had been sketching buildings and constructing fortresses. For Sawyer, attending the Coast Guard Academy and becoming an officer had been a deeply held ambition ever since he was in grade school. Being able to achieve his heart's desire had been one of the greatest moments in his life. He wanted nothing less for Daniel.

"Something tells me you'd be a great architect, Daniel. You're very talented," Ava gushed. Daniel was grinning from ear to ear. Ava's words made him want to sweep her up in his arms and plant a wet one right on her cheek. Daniel didn't get a lot of compliments outside of family members. His self-esteem was a huge issue because of neighborhood bullies and insensitive remarks from random strangers. Leave it to Ava to make him feel as if he could take the world by storm.

While the kids continued to work on the sand castle, Sawyer edged closer to Ava, intent on having a private word with her out of earshot of the children.

"Thanks for what you said to Daniel. He doesn't hear praise like that too often," he said in a low voice. Ava's act of kindness served as a reminder to him to continue to lift his brother up whenever possible. Positive reinforcement was a powerful motivator.

"You don't have to thank me. I meant every word of it. Daniel is creative and quite talented."

"I know, but sometimes people tend to focus on his limitations rather than his strengths."

Ava's eyes opened wide and she made a tutting noise. "Well, hopefully Daniel's success will just show them how small-minded they really are. It's unfair to count him out before he's even traveled down that road."

"I'm a firm believer in going after your dreams. There's no guarantee he'll become an architect, but he's got the talent and the vision to follow through with it."

"No, there are no guarantees," Ava conceded. "He might end up working in that field or become an artist or an architect's assistant. You just don't know where his dreams will take him."

Sawyer nodded in agreement. Most people didn't re-alize Daniel's potential. Because of Daniel's disability a lot of people assumed his brother would be greatly limited in his options. Ava was one of the few people who seemed to realize that Daniel's talent and vision were infinite. She didn't view his challenges as insur-mountable obstacles. Just knowing how deeply Ava be-lieved in his brother caused a groundswell of emotion to surge up inside him.

"Are you two going to just stand there talking?" Dolly asked as she wiped her brow with the back of her hand. "Building sand castles is hard work."

"It's hot out here, Sawyer. I'm a little thirsty," Dan-iel announced.

"Me, too," Casey piped up. More times than not, Casey always tended to be in agreement with Daniel. Sawyer suspected that the six-year-old thought Daniel hung the moon.

"If everyone's hungry, I can whip up some sandwiches at my place and bottles of water," he suggested, looking toward Ava to see if she was agreeable.

The kids all began speaking at once and talking over one another, delighted at the idea of having lunch at the lighthouse and spending even more time together.

Ava smiled and nodded. "I wouldn't dare say no at this point. I think I'd have a rebellion on my hands."

After gathering up all the beach toys, they walked down the beach toward the lighthouse. Along the way they made a game of collecting the most beautiful seashell. Casey let out a cry as he came upon the empty shell of a horseshoe crab. It was decided by unanimous vote that Casey had found a unique seashell. Rather than bring it with him, Casey gingerly placed it back in the ocean.

When they reached the lighthouse, he couldn't help stopping and admiring his new home. For some reason unknown to even him, he never got tired of the sight of it. The red-and-white-striped lighthouse stood in stark contrast to the deep blue sky. From the first time he'd laid eyes on it when he was a boy, it had been embedded in his heart and soul. He'd studied it, photographed it and explored its every nook and cranny. And all these years later it felt right to be the owner.

As he led the group into his house, Daniel took the lead and began showing Dolly and Casey around. Despite the fact that the twins had regularly visited Mr. P and knew the lighthouse like the back of their hand, they let out a few oohs and ahhs as they walked around. Mr. P had spent a lot of time and money renovating the lighthouse before his illness impacted his mobility. Although there were some changes Sawyer wanted to make to the master bedroom and the kitchen, he considered himself fortunate to not have to do a major overhaul of his living quarters.

"Is peanut butter and jelly still a crowd favorite?" He tossed the question out there as he headed toward the kitchen.

"That would be perfect. Thanks, Sawyer." Ava had followed behind him. She was looking around her with wonder, pausing to study a few unique aspects of his new digs. She ran her fingers along the copper stove he'd just had installed. A smile lit up her face as she opened up one of his cabinets and spotted the antique wall safe behind the door. As kids they'd been fascinated by the safe, spinning tales of unimaginable treasures hidden inside—gold coins, stacks of money and jewels had been some of their favorites.

"I think I might have some chicken salad in the fridge for a more refined palate," he said in a teasing voice.

She looked at him as if he were crazy. "Refined? Are you serious? Most days I eat what the kids are having…chicken nuggets, fries, hot dogs. And, of course, peanut butter and jelly. Being a mom has forced me to be flexible."

He shook his head knowingly. "Sounds exactly like what Daniel chows down on these days. Mom says he's eating them out of house and home." Although his mother complained about his brother's voracious appetite, Sawyer knew how much she enjoyed nurturing Daniel. He was, and always would be, her baby.

"He's such a sweetheart, Sawyer. The kids love spending time with him." Ava's gaze traveled toward the living room where Daniel and the twins were playing a spirited game of checkers.

"Well, he's like a big kid himself. It's tough for him to make friends his own age. He's just not on the same page with most twenty-year-olds." He pulled a loaf of bread and peanut butter from the cupboard. After rummaging around the refrigerator, he hit pay dirt with a jar of grape jelly.

"Success!" he said triumphantly, earning a chuckle from Ava.

"You're really making this place your own, aren't you?" she asked, a smile hovering on her lips.

He nodded, acknowledging she was right. "Yes, I suppose I am. At first I couldn't help thinking of it as Mr. P's place, but with every day that passes it's becoming more and more my own." He felt a burst of pride when he thought about his decision to buy the lighthouse. While some might call it impulsive, it was one of the best decisions he'd made in his life. It was the first place he'd owned lock, stock and barrel, and it came with a rich and textured Cape Cod history.

Ava leaned across the kitchen counter and began helping him make the sandwiches. "Mr. P would be happy about you living here. He always worried about finding a caretaker for this place. Then when he got sick and went downhill so quickly, there was no time to find anyone. Up until the very end he felt incredibly blessed to have lived such a long life here in Buzzards Bay."

Ava's voice was tinged with sadness, although it was

clear their friend had live a full, rich life. She and Mr. P had shared an amazing friendship. Even when they were kids, he'd always suspected Ava was Mr. P's favorite. And who could blame him? he thought. She'd always been kind and thoughtful, with a dash of playfulness most had found irresistible. He knew he'd never been able to resist Ava's adorable smile, infectious grin and her generous heart.

"It's a blessing to be back home. Living here—" He gestured around him with his hands. "It's icing on the cake."

"Cake? Are we having cake?" Casey asked, having heard the tail end of their conversation as he walked up. Within seconds, Dolly and Daniel began chattering about having cake for lunch. The din was so loud Sawyer felt the need to let loose with a loud whistle to calm things down.

When the kids quieted, he announced, "There is no cake, guys. But if you three want to sit down at the table for lunch, we made peanut butter and jelly sandwiches. And we have some chips." The kids let loose with groans of disappointment, still focused on cake.

Sawyer frowned at the children. Ava put her hand up to her mouth, trying unsuccessfully to camouflage her laughter. A flutter began rattling around his insides at the way her face lit up with merriment. He placed the food down in front of the kids, letting them know with the sternest look he could muster not to bring up cake again. Their dejected faces did a number on him. He let out a sigh, realizing he was nothing but a big pushover.

"I do have some double chocolate chip cookies I

bought at Ella's bakery." Judging by the exuberant reaction, Aunt Ella's double chocolate chip cookies held
the same sway as cake. Although his attention should
have been focused on the children, who were chanting
his name in celebratory fashion, it was a petite, dark-
haired woman with hazel eyes, grinning from ear to ear,
whom he couldn't seem to take his eyes off.

Ava kept finding new and interesting mementos scattered around the lighthouse. While Sawyer was engag-
ing the kids in a lively game of Battleship, she was
exploring his new home. In the living room, Sawyer had
played up the nautical theme, hanging lanterns from the
ceiling and using a vintage life preserver as wall décor.
He'd put in a beautiful, floor-to-ceiling white bookcase,
filled with books, photos and large conch shells. Sawyer's gold compass sat on the shelf. It had been his most
precious possession when they were children.

Whenever he'd been asked why he carried it around
with him wherever he went, he'd saucily replied, "Because I'm going places."

And he had gone places. All over the world, in fact.
One of the photos practically jumped out at her from
the shelf. It was a picture of Sawyer surrounded by a
group of beautiful African children. She carefully took
the frame off the shelf, wanting to get a closer look at
what had kept Sawyer away for almost a full year. The
huge smiles on their faces demonstrated their affection
for him. They were all dressed in brightly colored shirts
and American baseball caps. Sawyer's body language

spoke volumes. His arms lovingly encircled the kids, a look of contentment etched on his face.

"That photo was taken after my first month in Sierra Leone. It was taken in a town called Kailuhan."

Sawyer had quietly snuck up behind her, his voice like a warm breeze in her ear. "You have no idea how homesick I was, until I met this group of children. The coast guard brought boxes of baseball caps with us, knowing that kids overseas love them. You should have seen their faces when we handed them out. The gratitude was overwhelming. Can you believe most of these kids are orphans?"

Her heart sank. "That's terribly sad." She couldn't imagine children navigating their way through life without at least one parent. Somehow it put things into perspective about her own kids. Thankfully, she was still around to guide and nurture them. Even though she'd been an adult when her own parents passed away, it had still been a painful blow.

"They're still the most upbeat, positive bunch of kids I've ever been around. Despite suffering devastating losses, their land torn apart by war and living in poverty, they still have their faith and their love for one another."

"True faith endures." Time and time again, her father had uttered those words. Even in his darkest hours when cancer had taken his wife and invaded his own body, he'd still believed. And despite everything, he'd regarded each day as a gift.

Sawyer reached over and tapped the glass frame with

his finger. "This mission here…it's what I'm most proud of as a member of the coast guard. No question."

A poignant feeling swept over her. No doubt Sawyer would have other missions like this one in his future. Although they'd fallen into old patterns since his return from overseas, she still harbored doubts as to whether Sawyer would stick around for the long haul. He was young, motivated and an asset to the coast guard. Why shouldn't he travel the world and go where he was needed? There were plenty of trouble spots around the globe in need of heroes.

Holding this picture in her hands served as a painful reminder of Sawyer's absence this past year. Without him she'd had to forge on after becoming accustomed to his strong, steady presence. She hadn't allowed herself to wallow in self-pity, not with two children depending on her to be upbeat and strong. In the hours between darkness and dawn, she'd allowed herself to vent her sorrow in the privacy of her bedroom.

Now she was getting used to him being around all over again. He was fantastic with the kids. They sparkled whenever he was around. The love he felt for them was genuine, no doubt an extension of his love for Billy. What would it feel like to lose his larger-than-life presence? All this time she'd been fretting over how she'd feel if Sawyer left Cape Cod again. She knew there were plenty of other ways to lose him. How would she feel if he got married? If he fell in love? If she truly lost him?

A wave of sadness washed over her as an image of Sawyer coupled up with a beautiful young woman flashed into her mind. There was no use denying it. It would be agony when the time came for him to fall in love and get married. Oh, she knew she owed him better than that after everything he'd done for her family. She should want him to find happiness. But the truth was, it would hurt to see him settle down with someone else. It would burn her insides like acid. It would feel as if life as she knew it would never be the same.

Why? Because he'd always been her Sawyer. And she didn't want to share him. Because the very idea of him falling in love and getting married made her sick to her stomach. And jealous. And unsettled. Of course he'd had a few girlfriends over the years, and even then, she hadn't wanted to think of them as permanent fixtures in his life. Why hadn't she wanted him to find the One? Why had she always pushed the very idea out of her mind?

Chapter Eight

Deliteful Bakery, nestled in a small brick building among the quaint shops on Ocean Street, was a busy place to frequent on a Saturday morning. Ava was sitting in a corner table by the window, watching the organized chaos around her. It was nice to see Ella in her element—chatting with customers, decorating cupcakes and educating people about the benefits of all-natural products. The twins were having a ball icing cupcakes and decorating them with sprinkles.

Every Saturday Ella offered the kids in town a cupcake decorating class, complete with take-home treats. It was a win-win situation for the bakery. It got people into the shop while earning it a reputation as a kid-friendly establishment. Over the past six months, Ella had built quite a reputation for her bakery. Ava admired the way Ella had taken a simple idea and quickly turned it into a reality. The shop was doing so well, she'd recently been able to hire a part-time worker.

"I don't care what she says," Sunny muttered through

a mouthful of food. "These cupcakes must be loaded with sugar. They're scrumptious."

Ava shook her head at her sister. No matter how many times Ella assured her that the ingredients were low sugar and all natural, Sunny remained a skeptic. Sometimes she wondered whether she was simply messing with Ella, who at times could be tightly wound about her recipes.

In three quick strides, Ella was standing by their table, her hand perched on her hip. "I heard that!" she huffed, glaring at Sunny. "Please keep your conspiracy theories to yourself."

"What?" Sunny asked, all innocence and light. "It was a compliment. Your cupcakes taste as if they're a thousand calories."

"Earth to Sunny. It's not good for business to have my sister questioning the integrity of my ingredients."

Ava held her hand up. After spending a lifetime refereeing her sisters' squabbles, she knew the signs of trouble brewing.

"Ella," she interrupted, deftly changing the subject. "Before I forget, did the kids put in a cupcake order?"

Ella took a deep breath and exhaled. She turned to Ava and gave her a tense smile. "Yes, they did. That was their first order of business when they came in the shop today. I've boxed up half a dozen cupcakes for you to take with you. I put a candle on one of them."

Before she could thank Ella, Sunny jumped in. "Is it someone's birthday?"

Ava paused for a moment, knowing her sister would be all over her once she spilled the beans. "It's Sawyer's birthday. The kids wanted to bring him birthday cupcakes."

Sunny grinned and took a big gulp of her tea. "Well, bless their hearts," she drawled. "Are you making him dinner? Did you buy him a special gift? Or are you going to put him out of his misery and finally go out on a date with him?"

Ella signaled for her new employee to take over with the kids, then pulled out a chair and sat down, rolling her eyes in Sunny's direction. "They're just friends. How many times does she have to tell you that?" Ella swiveled her head in Ava's direction. "You are just friends, right?"

All of a sudden she felt tongue-tied. Her sisters were both staring at her, curiosity stamped on their faces. Yes, they were friends. But the feelings he incited in her as of late were more than platonic. Lately, she felt almost tongue-tied in his presence. "It's complicated," she said feebly.

"Aha. I knew it!" Sunny said in a spirited voice.

"Of course the two of us are friends, but lately, whenever we're together I get this fluttery, nervous feeling. I guess you could call it butterflies." She crinkled up her nose. "We've been friends for so long. It's strange to have this awareness of him as…you know, a man."

"You'd be crazy not to think of him that way. He's a tall, gorgeous coast guard hero. And every time he looks at you, those eyes of his are so intense and soulful." Sunny heaved a tremendous sigh.

"I've been running from these feelings for a long time, mostly because he's Billy's cousin. And Troy is full of disapproval whenever he sees Sawyer and me together. I never wanted to ruffle any feathers," she admitted with a rueful twist of her lips. "It hasn't done me any good. They're still here."

"If you keep running from it, you'll never know if there's something worth pursuing," Ella warned. "And you can't help who you're drawn to, sis. It makes perfect sense since you and Sawyer share such a rich history."

"Yes, but Troy and Nancy… They mean the world to me. And their feelings matter."

"But their feelings shouldn't trump your own…or Sawyer's," Sunny added.

Ava wrapped her hands around her mug of cappuccino. Even discussing this with her sisters was making her feel slightly self-conscious. After all, they weren't in a relationship, and they'd only shared that one kiss. Sawyer had gone out of his way the other day to dismiss it, calling it an impulsive gesture. Why didn't she believe him, though? Why did she think he was a lot more affected by that kiss than he was admitting? Because it had so deeply resonated with her it was hard to believe he hadn't felt something.

"First of all, other than that one kiss—" she started.

"You kissed him?" Ella interrupted, her eyes wide with surprise.

Sunny let out an indelicate snort. "Humph! I'm not one to say I told you so, but I told you so."

"We kissed last year. It was just one time, but it was romantic and tender. As far as kisses go, it was wonderful. But it was awkward afterward. Neither of us said a word about it. And the next thing you know he's leaving for a mission in Africa." She poked out her lower lip. "Not exactly a rousing endorsement."

Sunny waved her hand in the air. "Don't get stuck on the past. Live in the here and now. If you feel something for Sawyer, don't let fear hold you back."

"Do you have any idea how happy the twins are since he's been back?" She looked back and forth between her sisters. "He fills a void in their lives. No one could ever take their father's place, but they do benefit from having a strong male presence around. It makes them happy. Who am I to complicate things?"

She shook her head as images of Sawyer playing with the twins raced through her mind. "For so long he's been my best friend. I just don't know if it's smart to—"

"To what? Fall in love?" Ella asked with a raised eyebrow. "To put yourself out there again and risk it all for a chance to find that special someone?"

Ella's words rolled through her like a clap of thunder. Was that what was holding her back? Fear of falling in love?

Just then the twins came running over to the table with beautifully decorated cupcakes in hand. She, along with her sisters, began making a fuss over their decorating skills. Their faces lit up with pleased expressions as the compliments flowed. Within a few minutes the three of them were headed out the door, a box of cupcakes in hand as they walked down Ocean Street. As the twins ran ahead to look at the antique carousel, her mind wandered to the conversation she'd just had with her sisters. Ella hadn't pulled any punches. It always came back to the same thing. Loss. And fear. And the overwhelming anxiety she felt about losing another person she loved.

At some point she had to decide which was scarier—pushing past the fear of losing Sawyer or living a lifetime of regret.

"This was an awesome birthday surprise." It wasn't often Sawyer found himself getting choked up, but the artistically decorated cupcakes, the colorful balloons and the trip to the marina touched his heart.

More than anyone, Ava knew how much he loved boats and Buzzards Bay Harbor. It was at this very spot he'd seen his first coast guard cutter gliding across the water like a rocket. His life had never been the same once he'd laid eyes on the men in uniform—rugged, strong, patriotic—it had been the genesis of his career.

"The cupcakes were our idea, but Mama thought we should bring you down here." Dolly looked extremely proud of herself.

He reached out and tousled her windswept hair. More and more she was beginning to resemble her mother, with her sweet smile, gentle nature and an ability to make his insides melt. A heartbreaker in the making if he'd ever seen one.

"She said there's nothing you like better than boats," Casey added as he licked the frosting off his cupcake.

"Your mom knows me well," he answered, his gaze settling on Ava, who was seated across from him at the table. She was bundled up in a sweatshirt and wearing a pair of skinny jeans, looking as youthful as a teenager. He was glad he'd been wearing a long-sleeved shirt. Even in summertime it tended to get chilly down by the waterfront.

"It's the least we could do after everything you've done for the kids. And me." Her voice had a tender quality as she announced, "Happy birthday, Sawyer."

When he'd woken up this morning, it had been his intention to have a talk with Ava and clear the air. He was tired of holding back and keeping things from her. It was weighing heavily on him. Ever since his return he'd been putting it off, telling himself that he didn't want to sour things so quickly after his return. There were the children to consider, after all. There was no denying the cold, hard fear that rose within him whenever he thought about that awful night and the sight of his cousin lying cold and lifeless in the morgue. Would he really be doing the right thing by bringing back all those memories and laying them at Ava's feet? What was he supposed to say anyway? *"Excuse me, Ava, but I need to tell you something I should have told you two years ago."*

Colby had called him crazy when he finally confided in him about his argument with Billy, then divulged his plans to come clean with Ava. He'd accused him of wanting to put obstacles between the two of them.

Colby had said Sawyer didn't think he deserved her. He hadn't taken too kindly to his friend's off-the-wall comments. It was the closest they'd come in their years of friendship to an actual argument. In the end, they'd smoothed things over, each apologizing for getting heated. As a result of Billy's death, he'd learned not to let angry words cloud his judgment. There was no way he could ever walk away from Colby with anger in his heart. Not after what he'd already lived through.

And now his entire plan had fallen apart. Ava and the twins had shown up at the lighthouse, bursting into a chorus of "Happy Birthday" as soon as he opened the door. Without a word of explanation, they'd whisked him off to Ava's car, then to the marina, where a table had been set up for them to celebrate. Their birthday surprise had floored him, reaching a place inside him that longed to belong to something greater than himself.

Being gone for a year had changed him. It had taken his trip to the other side of the world to make him realize what he really and truly wanted in his life. A family of his own. Lately, he'd been wishing for things that had always seemed as elusive as catching lightning in a bottle.

For most of his adult life he'd enjoyed pleasant but brief relationships that hadn't gone anywhere. Those experiences left him feeling empty inside. Deep down, he'd always wanted a wife, someone who would love and cherish him through all the bad times, rejoicing with him during the good ones. He wanted kids. Enough to fill up a decent-size house, in fact. It didn't matter to him whether they were adopted or if they came from his wife's womb. He would love them all unconditionally.

"Can we go see the boats now?" Casey had gotten up from the table, his face full of eagerness as he stared at the boats lined up by the dock.

"Sure thing," Ava said. "It's why we came down here, right?"

As they made their way along the walkway, Sawyer

pointed out his favorite boats, pausing to talk to some of the fishermen and boat owners. One of the fishermen had caught a striped sea bass and was proudly displaying it in front of his boat. Casey and Dolly squealed with excitement, although Dolly hid behind his legs and peeked out at the fish, not wanting to get as up close and personal as her brother. It felt nice to have Dolly trust him enough to know he would protect her. And he would, he realized. With his very life.

Tonight had turned into a wonderful evening. Although he still had a niggling sensation in the pit of his stomach, he'd been able to largely ignore it and focus on the here and now. Because of his birthday celebration, he'd been given a reprieve. It wouldn't last forever, though. Sooner or later, he would have to sit down with Ava and bare his soul to her.

When the kids spotted Fresh Catch's boat they raced toward it, jumping aboard as soon as they saw Doug standing on deck. Sawyer deliberately slowed down his pace, his tone conversational as he turned toward Ava. "I've been meaning to tell you that the papers have all been signed for the sale of Trask boating. It's officially been sold."

She let out a huge sigh. "I have to admit I'm relieved. I know Trask boating meant a lot to you and Billy, but there was no way I could step in and take his place. What I know about boats could fit on a postage stamp."

Sawyer chuckled. Although Ava had always been supportive of their endeavor, she'd had very little to do with the running of the company. It had always been Billy's dream rather than his own. With his full-time coast guard duties, he simply didn't have the time or the energy to make a success out of it. "I'll drop off a check as soon as the lawyer sends me the paperwork. It will be a nice chunk of change to put in the bank."

Ava nodded along with his words. "It will be great to build up my savings. At the moment I feel very blessed to be able to stay at home with the twins, but sooner or later I'm going to have to go back to work."

Sawyer frowned. He'd never even thought about Ava's financial situation. Was everything all right on that end? He knew there had been some insurance money and a savings account, but he'd never asked about her finances. It would have felt too much like prying.

"Is everything okay on that front? I mean…is there anything I can do to help out?" he asked.

"We're fine, especially now that the company has been sold," she said. "We have some savings and the money from the life insurance policy, but that money won't last forever. I have to plan for the future. Braces. Summer camp. College tuition. At some point I have to have money coming in. I think I'm ready to get back to work."

He felt a burst of admiration for her. Knowing Ava as well as he did, he knew she was prepared to do whatever was necessary in order to care for her family. With all the talent and creativity she possessed, reviving her party planning business wouldn't be difficult. Her comment about being a stay-at-home mom made him wonder if she ever treated herself to a night out with friends. Although she was clearly a dedicated mother, she still needed time away from her children. Doing so would give her a chance to connect with adults and unwind. With a coast guard event drawing near, he might just have the perfect way to get Ava out of the house. "Hey, before I forget, do you have any plans for the night of the Fourth?"

"Nothing special. We usually just watch the fireworks from the patio. Dolly has an aversion to loud noises, so we skip the parades and the fanfare."

He crossed his arms across his chest, rocking back on his heels. At the moment he was acting on impulse, something he'd been doing a lot of lately. "The coast guard is having a party down at Sandy Neck. It's strictly for grown-ups. Would you like to come?"

Ava's eyes widened, and a surprised expression flashed across her face. "I don't know, Sawyer. It's been a while since I've done the social scene."

"Maybe that's the perfect reason for you to come hang out with us," he reasoned. "I know how much you love the kids, but you need to get out more often. The twins might like a break, as well," he teased.

"You sound like Sunny," she grumbled. "She thinks I'm the most boring person on the planet."

He let out a deep-throated laugh. "Well, prove her wrong. Come to the party. Good food, great music." He pointed to himself. "Not to mention great company."

Ava laughed and nodded. "Who could resist all that? Okay, I'll come."

"Great. Be there at seven," he said. "By the way, thanks for my birthday surprise." He leaned in and brushed a kiss against her forehead, his hands braced on either side of her face. She tilted her head upward, her expression registering surprise. The sudden impulse to place his lips on hers came over him, and he had to force himself not to follow his instincts. Instead, he took a step back, retreating from his up-close-and-personal view of her perfectly shaped pink lips.

She studied him, her eyes full of questions. "Sawyer, did you just ask me on a date?"

If her face hadn't been so serious, he might have laughed out loud. How could he tell her he wasn't even sure himself? All he knew for sure was he loved spending time with her. Ava made him feel things no other woman had ever kindled inside him. Being with her felt as natural as drawing breath.

"It's whatever we want it to be, Ava," he answered, his heart hammering a wild rhythm within his chest.

The beginnings of a grin began with the slight curving upward of her mouth, ending in a radiant, luminous smile. Relief flooded him. He'd gone out on a limb, putting himself out there to Ava in a way that he'd never done before. This was about way more than an enduring friendship. It was about possibilities. A feeling of euphoria washed over him, and he felt more free than he had in a very long time. And even though he knew he still had unfinished business with Ava, he just wanted to savor this perfect moment, even though it was only a reprieve. Soon enough he would have to face the music.

On Wednesday night, Ava was returning home after attending a fund-raiser meeting for the twins' school. She'd enlisted Sunny to babysit the twins so she could participate. She couldn't stop smiling as she drove down Ocean Street and then made the winding turn onto Sea Glass Lane. The mood in the meeting had been light and friendly, supportive and full of laughter. It hadn't been awkward at all. Most of the faces were new to her, but a few were friends from high school who she hadn't seen in ages. She let out a contented sigh. Although she'd felt unconnected to the townsfolk of Buzzards Bay for a very long time, the tide was beginning to turn. A feeling of satisfaction thrummed through her veins. She tapped her fingers against the steering wheel to the beat of the hit song on the radio.

Community. For so long now she'd taken her own community for granted. Her whole life she'd been blessed to have strong ties with the residents of Buzzards Bay and the congregation of Sea Street Church. She'd never had to worry about fitting in or being different. There had been no doubt she'd belonged to this town and its people. Pastor Felix, her sisters and Sawyer had all been right. Cutting herself off from her congregation and the folks in town had only led to her feeling disconnected and unhappy. She needed them, not only as a sounding board and a support system, but as a bridge between her and Sea Street Church.

Perhaps this was the first step in finding her way back to worship. Meeting the other mothers was an eye-opening experience. Oftentimes, she felt as if she were the only one going through the loss of a spouse or raising children without a husband by her side. That was the furthest thing from the truth. Tonight she'd met a woman named Peggy who'd not only lost her husband but had four children to support and nurture. All things considered, Ava felt a sense of gratitude wash over her.

When she pulled into her driveway, the house was lit up like a Christmas tree. Lights blazed from every window, including Dolly's and Casey's bedrooms. It was strange considering the twins had a bedtime of eight o'clock. The clock on her dashboard confirmed it was well past nine. It wasn't like Sunny to disregard her wishes regarding the children. After parking her car she glanced down at her cell phone. Eight missed calls! Panic skittered along her nerves. She'd turned her cell phone off before the meeting started and had forgotten to turn it back on. A burst of adrenaline flooded her and she ran toward her house, charging through the door as if her feet were on fire.

Sawyer, Casey, Dolly and Sunny were calmly sitting around the kitchen table. Relief flooded her at the sight of her children safe and sound. Casey was sipping from an oversize mug while Dolly was munching on a chocolate chip cookie. Both of them gazed at her with wide, innocent eyes.

"What are you two doing up? Lights-out was over an hour ago." She frowned at her sister. Sunny scowled right back at her.

"There was a little…incident," her sister said. Sawyer glanced over at Casey, then shot her a look filled with meaning.

"What do you mean? What happened?" Her voice rang out more strident than she'd intended.

"Casey snuck out of the house after lights-out and Auntie Sunny got scared really, really bad," Dolly piped up. "And I got frightened, too, because it was getting dark outside."

"Casey! What in the world were you thinking?" she asked as she struggled to make sense of her son's disobedience.

Casey looked at her with fear shimmering in his eyes. He ducked his head down and mumbled, "I wanted to go see Uncle Sawyer. I had to ask him something really important. And Aunt Sunny said it was too late since it was bedtime."

She shot a grateful look in her sister's direction. "Auntie was right. You should have listened to her. And you can't just show up at Uncle Sawyer's house anytime you please."

"When I arrived home after my shift, I saw this little guy sitting on my front steps waiting for me," Sawyer explained. "I almost couldn't believe my eyes."

For a moment she was speechless. Even though Sawyer's lighthouse was only a short walk down the beach, it frightened her to think of her child walking along a deserted stretch of beach at night. Buzzards Bay was a safe haven, but even the best communities had their fair share of trouble. And even though she welcomed Sawyer into their lives with open arms, she didn't want either of her children treating him as a part of their everyday lives. As it was, they were drawn to him like a beacon. Even when they weren't in his presence, they were talking about being with him. She needed to sit the kids down and set some boundaries. That way it wouldn't be so painful when the day came for Sawyer to settle down with someone and start his own family.

Painful for whom? a little voice whispered. *The twins? Or yourself?*

Arms folded across her chest, she addressed her son. "I can't believe you would go against your aunt's wishes and our house rules," she snapped. "Casey Trask, march yourself upstairs to bed after apologizing to Aunt Sunny and Uncle Sawyer."

Casey mumbled apologies as tears gathered in his eyes. His expression hinted at defiance.

"Mommy, are we still going to the fair tomorrow?" Dolly asked.

"After tonight I'm not making any promises," she said in a no-nonsense tone, her mind still whirling with her son's antics. "It's not my style to reward bad behavior."

"That's not fair! I didn't sneak out of the house. He did," Dolly shouted. She pointed a pudgy finger in Casey's direction. "It's all your fault!"

"No, it's not my fault," he screamed back at her. "If Mom just married Uncle Sawyer I wouldn't have to sneak out after dark to see him. I could see him anytime I want!"

Chapter Nine

If Mom just married Uncle Sawyer I wouldn't have to sneak out after dark to see him.

Casey's statement left a hush over the room. Ava's cheeks were flushed, although he couldn't tell whether it was from anger or embarrassment. Sunny's mouth hung open. Even Dolly was left speechless. He experienced a myriad of emotions. First and foremost, he felt a spark of joy that Casey thought so highly of him. He had to tell himself not to grin from ear to ear, especially since Ava looked so bent out of shape about it.

"It's definitely past your bedtime," Sunny announced as she grabbed each twin by the hand and hustled them out of the room. Groans and mumbles echoed in their wake.

"I—I don't know where that came from," Ava stammered. "Where would he ever get an idea like that?"

Sawyer shrugged. "Where does any of it come from? The imagination of a six-year-old boy. Don't stress about it."

She chewed her lip. "I can't imagine what's gotten

into him tonight. Sneaking out of the house, being so incredibly disobedient and then trying to play matchmaker with us." She ran her hand through her shoulder-length hair. "I'm going to have to put my foot down and punish him. Otherwise he'll think I'm a pushover. Maybe he'll have to miss out on the fair this year."

Even though Ava was trying to sound as tough as nails, he could see the telltale signs of vulnerability. Her lips were trembling. Just the idea of making Casey miss the annual fair was doing a number on her. Sawyer saw all the doubt and worry reflected back at him. His heart constricted.

He reached out and gently placed his hand on her shoulder. Their eyes locked. Something in their depths made him pull her into his arms so that she could rest her head against his chest. He closed his eyes as she settled into the crook of his arm. A desire to protect her rose within him. He couldn't stand seeing her so disheartened. Releasing her, he held her at arm's length so he could look her directly in the eye.

"Ava, don't you remember all the times we sneaked out past curfew so we could explore the beach at low tide?"

"But that was diff—" She stopped herself midsentence.

"Different?" he asked. "Not really. Casey's not much younger than we were. We called ourselves explorers. Adventurers. Maybe he's a chip off the old block."

Ava shook her head and let out a soft chuckle. "When you put it that way, it seems like no big deal. But it still doesn't feel right." A sigh slipped past her lips. "Casey's been going against the rules for months now. I think he's testing me."

"Or maybe he's just being a kid."

She blinked and seemed surprised by his words. Her expression eased up a bit, and she nodded. "Or maybe he's just being a kid," she acknowledged.

"I hate to bail on you, but I've got to get some sleep," he said, covering his mouth with his hand as a yawn escaped. "I just worked a ten-hour shift and I'm wiped out. See you tomorrow, Ava."

He bent down and placed a kiss on her forehead, his lips lingering for an instant longer than necessary. A fruity scent rose to his nostrils.

"I'm not making any promises about tomorrow," she answered, her eyebrows drawn together in a mock gesture of fierceness.

He winked at her, knowing he would indeed be seeing her at the fair. As he walked back toward his lighthouse, his thoughts began to drift back to Ava. She was a big part of his world, and with every day that passed she and the twins were becoming more and more important to him. He'd never dreamed the feelings he harbored could grow even stronger. But they had. Over the course of the past few weeks, they'd magnified and strengthened like an oak tree firmly planted in the soil. And he could try to fool himself into believing it was something he could stuff down inside him. But he would only be lying to himself. He could no longer deny the depth of emotion he felt toward her, the push and pull in his direction he experienced every time he was within a five-mile radius of her beautiful, radiant face.

Try as he might, he couldn't stop daydreaming about sharing another tender, wonderful kiss with Ava.

"Hey, are you two sure your mom won't mind you having another corn dog?" Sawyer was standing with the twins at the concession stand, his hands full of corn dogs, juice boxes and French fries. "I mean, I'm not the food police, but you've already had hamburgers, chips and ice cream. In a few hours this could get ugly."

Casey reached for his corn dog, his eyes wide with appreciation as he took a bite. Once he swallowed he answered, "We never get tummy aches. Our stomachs are made of steel."

Dolly took a bite of her corn dog, letting out a sigh of appreciation. "We did get sick that one time, remember, Casey?"

The twins exchanged a look filled with hidden meaning.

"Wonderful," he mumbled, wishing he'd cut them off before the corn dogs. "Your mom will be thrilled."

Rule number one in dealing with kids, he reminded himself. Always be the adult in the situation. He made a mental note to tell Ava about their food consumption when they caught up with her at the fair. That way there would be no surprises if they happened to have bellyaches later on. It was hard for him to say no to Casey and Dolly. For some reason he wanted to give them everything—toys, games, outings. Most of all, his love and attention.

If he could, he'd wrap the world up and hand it to them on a silver platter. On his part it was an attempt to make up for the void in their lives caused by their father's death. And to fulfill his promise to Billy. He was still figuring out how to play a significant role in their lives without overstepping the boundaries. Ava had made it perfectly clear last night that there needed to be limits.

He took a quick glance at his watch. "Hey, why don't we go find your mom's booth?" he suggested. "It's almost one o'clock."

The coast guard, along with Sea Street Church and half a dozen other businesses and organizations, had joined together to raise money for Habitat for Humanity. They'd set up their annual fair at Sandy Neck Beach, complete with concessions, games, rides and contests. One hundred percent of the proceeds would benefit the organization. He'd been overjoyed to find out from Ava that she was manning the booth for Sea Street Church, along with a few members of the congregation.

When they finally located her, she was talking with a few other volunteers and handling the cash box. With her pretty floral dress, sun hat and silver sandals, she stood out like a beacon in the darkness. She looked lighthearted. And happy. A far cry from the woman she'd been two years ago. Even though he knew she would still have moments of grief and sadness in the future, he felt very strongly that she'd turned a corner.

When she'd told him about helping out with today's event, he'd been overjoyed. Being a part of the church community would not only give support to Ava, but it would aid her on her spiritual journey.

"Mama!" Dolly cried as she spotted her mother and

took off running toward her. Dolly scooted behind the table and latched on to her leg. Casey played it cool and kept pace with Sawyer, choosing to give his mother a simple hand wave rather than anything demonstrative.

"Aren't you supposed to be at the coast guard booth?" Ava asked, her lips twitching in amusement. She reached out and grabbed a few French fries from his plate.

He nodded toward the food. "As you can see, we got sidetracked." He made a face. "I didn't realize two six-year-olds could eat so much."

Ava laughed and nuzzled the top of Casey's head. "Sorry about that. I forgot to tell you about their voracious appetites. They must be going through a growth spurt."

Growth spurts. Yet another thing he didn't have a clue about. "I should get going so I can relieve Hank. He basically agreed to this kicking and screaming." He rubbed his hands together gleefully. "I'm inviting you all to come on over to the coast guard booth and see if you can knock me down."

As a way of making money for the cause, the coast guard had set up a dunking booth. His shift began in five minutes. From what he'd seen earlier, the lines had been long and steady.

"That should be interesting." Ava had a twinkle in her eye. She fished around in her purse and produced a wad of bills. "What do you say, kids? Should we give it a shot?"

"Yes! Yes! We want to try," the kids responded enthusiastically, both of them talking over each other in their excitement.

As soon as they reached the coast guard booth, Sawyer spotted Hank sitting on the perch making faces at some of his buddies who were trying to unseat him. Next thing you knew, Hank was in the water and the crowd was cheering and pointing. As soon as he saw him, Hank motioned for Sawyer to replace him. Judging by the look on his face, he'd had enough.

Before he made his way over, he turned around toward Ava and the kids, casually tossing a comment in their direction before he walked away. "Hey, guys, on second thought, save your money. I have a feeling I won't be getting wet today." He raised his arm and flexed his muscles.

Ava rolled her eyes. "That's a mighty bold statement. Especially considering I was the pitcher for the Buzzard Bay All Stars. Or have you conveniently forgotten that fact?"

Sawyer hadn't forgotten a thing. As a twelve-year-old, Ava had been able to throw an amazing knuckleball. She'd led her team to two back-to-back undefeated seasons. Watching her pitch had been like experiencing a force of nature.

Sawyer waved his hand in the air. "Girls can't throw!" he taunted, deliberately trying to get Ava riled up. He loved it when she got a little feisty and competitive, the way she'd done when they were kids.

Dolly huffed and placed her hands on her hips. She was tapping her sneaker against the ground. "That is not true, Uncle Sawyer! I'm the pitcher on my baseball team and I'm good. Very good," she emphasized with a nod.

"She's a chip off the old block." Ava's voice was tinged with pride.

"It's true, Uncle Sawyer. Dolly is the best in our whole class, including me," Casey piped up.

Ava patted Dolly on the shoulder. "Don't worry. He's just trash-talking, trying to psyche us out before we take him down."

"You're going down!" Dolly warned. Her eyes gleamed with anticipation, and her lips were curved in a gleeful smile. Casey looked back and forth between the two camps. His eyes were huge, and he was biting his lip. Sawyer felt a pang when he realized Casey was having a hard time choosing sides. Sawyer winked at him, letting him know it was all in good fun. The little guy looked relieved as he stepped up to the counter.

As Sawyer settled himself on the perch, he made a funny face at Casey, earning him a stuck-out tongue. Casey tossed the four balls, not even coming close to hitting the target.

Dolly eagerly took her brother's place and stared Sawyer down with serious attitude. He forced himself not to smile, even though he could feel the corners of his mouth twitching in amusement. By the looks of it, Dolly meant business.

Even though he was rooting for her to hit the target, Dolly missed it each time by only a hair. Everyone began chanting Ava's name as she stepped forward and plunked her money down on the table. He barely had time to blink before the ball was whizzing toward him.

Just as he heard the thwacking sound of the ball hitting the target, he felt his seat giving way beneath him. As his body hit the cold water, he let out a cry of surprise. When he emerged from the water, Dolly was throwing her hand in the air, celebrating. Casey was jumping up and high-fiving his mom. His coast guard buddies were hooting and hollering. A warm feeling spread through his chest at the sight of the three of them laughing.

At the end of his shift, Ava was there waiting for him, towels in hand. Despite the warm midday sun, he was shivering from repeatedly being dunked in the water. He quickly dried himself, draping the towel around his neck when he finished.

"Thank you, Sawyer." The tone of her voice had him looking up to meet her gaze. The heartfelt look on her face had him melting like ice cream in the hot sun.

"For what?" He tried to keep his tone even, to pretend as if he didn't know what she was talking about.

"For trying to take my mind off Casey's disappearing act last night. For making me laugh. And for showing the kids such a good time. I appreciate it."

He let out a sigh and rolled his shoulders. "I guess I'm as subtle as a sledgehammer."

She reached out and touched his arm. "You're great. I know you're coming from a good place."

He met her gaze, trying to read her expression. It was important to tread lightly. "At the risk of sounding like a broken record, you're not alone in this."

Her face took on a somber expression. She shrugged, her slight shoulders making her look vulnerable. It was deceptive, since Ava was one of the strongest, most courageous women he'd ever known.

"If you need anything…or just want to talk, let me know. I'm here for you."

Ava's chin quivered. "Thanks. Casey told me this morning that he's been missing Billy more than usual." She wrapped her arms around her middle and looked down at the ground. "You know, they say time heals all wounds. I'm not so sure about that. Some days it seems as if it were just yesterday. Then other times I feel as if it's been forever since we last saw him."

Personally, he'd never liked the expression about time healing all wounds. From firsthand experience he knew that wasn't always the case. Time hadn't fully healed his broken heart when Billy and Ava had gotten married. Of course the pain had eased a bit over time. But he'd still had his heart kicked around, and it was debatable as to whether he still carried around some of those hurts.

"I think some wounds never fully go away. But they do heal, leaving a scar behind. Our scars tell us a story, of where we've been, what we've been through. That's how I like to look at it. We all have scars, Ava. You can't really go through life without getting 'em."

She sent a tender smile in his direction, her eyes full of gratitude. "That's how I feel sometimes. I'm healing, but scarred. So are the twins. There's this little hole in their hearts that might always be there. Sometimes it feels like everyone is dancing around me. Everybody wants me to be exactly who I was before the accident. I'm still me, but forever changed. Does that make sense?"

"It makes perfect sense. How could you possibly be the same woman after what you've endured?"

Ava nodded. "You get it, don't you? I don't know how or why, but you understand. And I'm grateful for that."

She reached out and squeezed his hand, causing him to think about how well her hand fit in his. A perfect fit. Of course he understood, although she had no way of knowing why. After nearly losing his life in Sierra Leone, he considered himself a changed man. Traumatic events left indelible marks in people's lives. Now he went out of his way to appreciate the things he'd always taken for granted. His relationship with the Lord was stronger, fortified under the most harrowing circumstances. Living the best possible life had new meaning. He considered himself to be truly blessed. Someday down the road, he hoped Ava would, too.

As far as Ava was concerned, spending time at the fair had been the perfect way to pass a summer's day. There had been so much laughter and joy today. As the activities wound down, she found herself on cleanup duty, packaging up items, gathering trash and picking up empty bottles and recyclable items from the sand. The goal of the volunteers was to leave the beach as pristine as they'd found it. Truthfully, she had to admit to herself that things were getting better as of late. She was feeling more upbeat, and her focus was on the here and now. She was finding joy in the simplest of things. A beautiful sunset. A walk on the beach. Casey's infectious laugh. Dolly tickling her senseless. With the kids heading off to a playdate with friends, she didn't have any plans for the rest of the day.

Earlier this morning she'd packed up the rest of the items in Billy's closet and dropped them off at a thrift store. The folks at the shop had been very grateful for her donation. Letting go of Billy's things made her feel as if a weight had been lifted from her chest. The sight of Sawyer lifting one of the wooden partitions, his powerful muscles flexing with every movement, drew her attention toward him.

As if he sensed her scrutiny, his gaze swung up to meet hers. There was something intense radiating from him. For a moment everything else fell away so that it seemed as if it were just the two of them. She wasn't sure she could handle what was reflected in his eyes. There was too much pent-up emotion she was battling. And so much uncertainty about her feelings for Sawyer.

She already felt a twinge of guilt about the way her mood had elevated the moment she'd spotted him. He made her feel safe and protected, as if nothing bad could happen on Sawyer's watch. He always brought a smile to her face. Perhaps it was the vibe of positivity he radiated. Or the way he made her chuckle at the simplest of things. She felt content. And hopeful about the future.

After unloading the partition Sawyer began making his way toward her, his stride full of power and certainty.

"Where are the kids?" Sawyer asked as he scanned the area in their proximity. "Please don't tell me they're off somewhere eating cotton candy."

"One of their classmates invited them over to their house to play, so I don't have to pick them up until later. They're going to be tuckered out when they get home."

The fact that they'd wanted to spend time at a friend's house made her happy. It had worried her to no end that the twins tended to stay at home rather than socialize with other kids. In the past few months they'd been spreading their wings more and more by venturing out of their comfort zone. And even though it ached a little bit to have them leave the nest, she was encouraging them to fly.

Sawyer's eyes roamed over her face as if he were trying to figure something out. "Ava, there's something I need to talk to you about."

The serious tone of his voice caused her to tense up. There was this wild feeling in the pit of her stomach, making her uneasy. She held up her hand to hold him off as a sliver of awareness crept along her spine. She knew that whatever he had to say might change things between them. For better, for worse. She couldn't be certain. Things might never be the same again.

Was he going to tell her he was leaving Buzzards Bay again? Would she once again have to deal with losing him? Or was he going to say something that might forever shift the dynamic between them? Either way, she wasn't ready for it. Not now. Not when she was flying so high on this happy, peaceful feeling.

"Don't, Sawyer," she blurted out. "You have such an intense look on your face. I can't handle anything heavy right now." She studied his body language, noticing the way his frame shuddered and sagged a little. "I'm sorry. This day has been so carefree, so enjoyable. I just want that feeling to last a little longer."

He nodded, his eyes hooded. "I understand." His

voice sounded a little hollow, and for a moment she wanted to take back her words and hear what he had to say. She felt a little selfish denying him a voice, but she hadn't planned on Sawyer discussing anything deep with her. What she was feeling caught her off guard. It started as ripples of awareness flowing through her. Now it was roaring inside her like a call to action. At this moment, more than anything, she wanted to celebrate being alive. Other than the twins, Sawyer was the one person in the world who made her want to lift her face toward the sun, raise her arms to the heavens and thank God for being able to wake up this morning.

"If you're finished here, can we just… Do you want to take a drive?" Unbidden, the words tumbled from her lips.

The look of utter surprise on Sawyer's face had her wishing she'd headed toward the safety of her car. For a few agonizing seconds she wondered if he was going to turn her down. A wide grin slowly began to take over his face as he nodded and reached for her hand.

"Where are we headed to?" he asked. All the tension evaporated and his face held a boyish expression.

"Barefoot Point Beach. I just want to get in my car and put the top down so I can feel the wind whipping through my hair. It's been a while."

"Let's do it." Sawyer led her by the hand down the hill toward where her car was parked. Located half an hour's drive from Buzzards Bay, it was the only beach in the area where you could find sea glass. As kids they hadn't ventured to Barefoot Point often, but when they did it had been a rare treat. It had been a family affair—

mothers, fathers, sisters, brothers—all of them spending the day swimming, picnicking, collecting seashells and basking in the sun.

Most of all, they'd all enjoyed hunting for spectacular sea glass. At the end of the day, their buckets had always been filled to the rim with a rainbow-colored assortment—sea blue, green, amber, topaz, crimson.

As she drove down the winding road toward the beach, she caught a glimpse of the brilliant blue ocean churning against the tide. Even from a distance she could make out figures hunched over on the beach collecting sea glass. At the sight of it joy bubbled up inside her. Few things made her feel like a little kid again, but this was certainly one of them. As she walked the beach with Sawyer, stopping every few feet to drop sea glass into their makeshift bucket, it turned into a joyous adventure.

"I'm looking forward to the Fourth," Sawyer said, reminding her of their plans. She made a mental note to make sure Nancy and Troy could still watch the kids. She bit her lip, wondering at their reaction when they discovered her Fourth of July plans were with Sawyer. No, she wasn't going to think about anything negative. Not now. Somehow today had turned into an unexpected gem. It was like one of those moments when you were walking on the beach and stumbled upon the perfect shell. When was the last time she'd done anything spontaneous? Something just for herself?

"I'm looking forward to it also," she murmured. "And, Sawyer, thanks for being there for me today. You've helped make this day special."

Rather than say a single word, he reached out and squeezed her hand, his eyes dark with things left unsaid. She couldn't explain, not even to herself, why it felt as if today was all about new beginnings.

Chapter Ten

"Thanks again for watching the kids tonight." Ava's in-laws had come over to the house so they could watch the twins for the evening while she was out. "They're so excited you're sleeping over."

"We love spending time with the grands, especially on Fourth of July." Nancy gestured toward the patio. "And we can watch the fireworks from outside. You have a wonderful view from up here."

Ava's mother-in-law was a petite, dark-haired beauty who looked years younger than her actual age. A fitness enthusiast, she claimed daily exercise kept her youthful. "So, where are you off to?" her father-in-law, Troy, asked. "You look mighty patriotic in that red, white and blue." Ava looked down at her white jeans and the blue-and-red-striped shirt she'd owned forever. She'd rummaged all through her closet looking for something special to wear this evening to showcase her love for the U.S.A.

"Sawyer invited me to a party at Sandy Neck Beach hosted by the coast guard."

Troy's body stiffened. His face hardened, the wrinkles near his eyes becoming more pronounced as he let out a low grunt. "You two seem to be spending a lot of time together," he huffed.

Her mother-in-law looked over at her husband. Her features were pinched. She seemed to be sending him a warning signal with her eyes.

"Does that upset you?" Ava asked, surprised at Troy's reaction. She had no intention of ignoring the elephant standing in the room, despite the tension crackling in the air. Although he'd hinted at his disapproval of her and Sawyer's friendship on several occasions, she couldn't remember Troy ever being so harsh.

"I just don't think it's proper for you to be dating Sawyer." He slashed his hand through the air. "There! I've said it. I have no problem with you wanting to move forward with your life. You're young and beautiful. But, as the saying goes, there's plenty of fish in the sea. You need to start fishing in another pond."

"Troy! That's enough!" his wife admonished. "It's not our business who Ava does or doesn't date."

"We're not dating," she interjected. "We're friends. Always have been." *But what if we were a couple?* She wanted to ask. *Would there really be an objection?*

He threw his hands in the air. "Call it what you like, but I've seen the way he looks at you. And I'm not blind to the way you look at him, either," he barked. "And pretty soon the children are going to start asking questions about Mommy and Uncle Sawyer." He tossed a pointed look in her direction before striding out of the kitchen.

Ava sucked in a shocked breath. She'd never had a cross word with Troy in her life, yet their conversation had been full of tension and none-too-subtle digs. Did her father-in-law really believe she'd carry on with Sawyer right under the twins' noses? The very thought wounded her. And did he think she was chasing after Sawyer like a dog hunting a bone? All that talk about fishing had her mind in a whirl.

Nancy made a tutting noise and shook her head at her husband's retreating figure. "I'm sorry for that display of bad manners. He knows better than to raise his voice like that at you."

"No need to apologize, Mom. He's always been a straight shooter. Why should this be any different?" She loved and respected Troy, and as confused as she felt about his outburst, she knew he'd never purposely try to hurt her. It was evident he'd been carrying around a lot of baggage since his son's death.

"Come and sit down, dear." Nancy patted the chair next to her, crossing her hands in front of her as Ava planted herself in the seat. "Troy has always been a bit protective of Billy. That hasn't changed a bit, even though he's no longer with us."

Ava frowned, not sure she understood Nancy's meaning. "Are you saying he's threatened by the idea of Sawyer and me being together?"

"Something like that. This may sound strange, but I think it's hard for him to accept that life goes on, even though Billy isn't part of it. He was his whole world, and now he's gone. So even though he's way out of line to act that way, this is the only way he can protect Billy."

She nodded, understanding flowing through her. "I get that. Believe me, I still feel protective of Billy's memory myself. And for a long time it seemed strange to me that life could go on without him." She stared out the bay window, marveling at the brilliant blue sky and the sun's dazzling shimmer. "I used to wonder how the sun could keep on shining without Billy."

"Or how the world kept turning on its axis." Nancy let out a sigh. "I know I've said this before, but it's a terrible thing to outlive your child."

Ava reached out and patted her hand. She'd witnessed Troy and Nancy's suffering over the past few years and she knew how profoundly Billy's death had shattered their world. As a mother, she could only imagine how it felt to lose your only child.

"We all have to move forward, though, don't we?" she asked. "We have to live."

She was saying it as much for herself as for her in-laws. For too long she'd been standing in one place without a clear road map for the future. That had to change. Treading water just wasn't enough anymore. She yearned to feel the urge to kick up her heels, to swim out past the buoys without fear of something happening to her.

"Forgive me for asking, but is there something going on between you and Sawyer?" Nancy's voice was tinged with curiosity, her eyes sparkled with interest. There was a hint of apprehension in her tone.

Ava knew her mother-in-law well enough to know

that whatever they discussed would remain in her strictest confidence. She'd never been one to judge, and she always gave people her true, honest opinions.

"If you'd asked me that question a few weeks ago, I would've said no. But lately…there's something more than friendship between us, but neither one of us has been able to deal with it head-on." She shrugged, feeling confused by the mix of emotions flowing through her. "I couldn't even put a name to it if I tried. I just know when I'm with him I feel more complete than I ever have before."

She quickly glanced over at Nancy's face, hoping she hadn't offended her by talking about her feelings for Sawyer.

"Mom, I didn't mean—" she began.

"Hush." Nancy said in a low voice as she reached over and squeezed her hand. "There's no question in my mind that you loved my Billy. Your devotion to him was unwavering. I know it wasn't always easy. You deserve to find happiness, Ava. More than anyone I've ever known. But if I'm being completely honest, the thought of you and Sawyer being together gives me pause. It would be very awkward for the family, especially considering how Troy feels. Not to mention that Dolly and Casey consider him a member of the family. He was like a brother to Billy."

Ava's eyes moistened. A lump formed in her throat. She cared so very much about her in-laws' feelings, and it hurt to know neither one of them would approve of a relationship between her and Sawyer. "I appreciate your honesty, even if it wasn't what I wanted to hear."

Since her own mother's death she'd leaned on Nancy as more than a mother-in-law. She was a friend and a confidante. Her life was a testament to the things she held dear—family, faith and friendship. Although no one could ever replace her own mother, Nancy had stepped in to fill that void. Ava loved her dearly. Her in-laws were one of the few links she had to Billy and the twins' only living grandparents. Alienating them would only serve to hurt her children. Hadn't they suffered enough loss?

"I feel sort of silly talking about this without even knowing how Sawyer feels," she backtracked. A little voice inside her had been telling her maybe she'd been imagining the spark of chemistry between her and Sawyer. Maybe this was all very one-sided. "Tonight sort of feels like a date, but I think we're both testing out the waters."

Nancy furrowed her brow. "Sounds like there's something brewing between the two of you. A woman always knows."

Trust your gut. It had been her mother's favorite saying.

"I couldn't love Sawyer any more if he was my own, but I can't condone something I don't think is right," Nancy continued, a twinge of regret in her voice. "Just play it smart, love. I'd hate to see the two of you ruin your wonderful friendship if you venture down that road and things don't work out. What do I know? I'm just a small-town girl at heart. Relationships have changed a lot since I fell in love with my honey. I couldn't imagine being with anyone else but Troy."

Nancy's last comment stung. Was she insinuating that Ava would be disloyal to Billy's memory if she pursued a relationship with Sawyer? Was that what Nancy really thought? Ava bit her lip, troubled by the idea of causing so much friction in the Trask family. Her mother-in-law was a wise woman. She'd spoken from the heart and held nothing back, even if it wasn't warm and fuzzy. She'd voiced Ava's own fears about any future she might have with Sawyer. What if things didn't work out? What if everything blew up in their faces? Would he still want to stick around? Or would she lose him the same way she'd lost him once before?

By the time seven o'clock rolled around, Sawyer was anxiously checking his watch and scanning the pavilion for any sign of Ava. He'd arrived at the party early to help set up, wanting to catch up with his team before the event started. In the year he'd been gone, there was a lot he'd missed out on—Hank had gotten engaged, Bridget and Toby were expecting and Paddy, his mentor, had put the papers in for his retirement. There was no way he could put into words how much he'd missed the camaraderie and loyalty they offered him on a daily basis. Colby. Hank. Bridget. Paddy. And Raoul. They'd always had his back, and he would always have theirs.

Once again, he scanned the area for Ava. Technically, this wasn't a date, but in many ways it felt like one. It was the first real opportunity he'd had to spend some one-on-one time with Ava in an intimate, grown-up atmosphere. Since he'd been back the twins had served as a buffer between them. Their moments of alone time had been few and far between. Excitement was building inside him at the thought of spending quality time together, the same way they had done at Barefoot Point Beach.

Colby sidled up to him, his blue eyes flashing with amusement. "You look as nervous as a fifteen-year-old on his first date."

Sawyer jabbed his best friend in the side with his elbow, eliciting a muttered cry.

"Easy there, big guy. I was just kidding."

"I'm not nervous, just excited to spend some time with her. She should have been here by now," he explained, his gaze shifting between Colby and the entrance. Raising his arm, he took a quick glance at his watch. It was quarter past seven and still no Ava.

Colby let loose with a low-throated chuckle. "You've got it bad."

A trickle of awareness crept up Sawyer's spine, just as he spotted Ava standing at the pavilion scanning the venue. Ava had dressed casually for the event, looking every inch the girl next door. Her dark hair was tied up in a short ponytail and wound with a red ribbon. She was decked out in red, white and blue. Perfect for the occasion. He reached her side in a few quick strides, slowing down at the end so as not to appear too eager. Colby was right, he realized. His actions reminded him of his adolescent self. Heart thundering in his chest. Restless energy. His mouth feeling dry.

The moment Ava spotted him, he detected a look of relief on her face. Even though she'd grown up in Buzzards Bay and knew most of the people in town, it had been several years since she'd been part of the social scene. Most of the time, she'd kept to herself, with the exception of her family and close friends. He imagined it was all part and parcel of her grieving process. It made him happy that she'd ventured out because of his invitation.

"Ava, it's good to see you." He leaned in and pressed a kiss on her cheek. The smell of vanilla wafted to his nostrils, and he inhaled deeply.

"Thanks for inviting me." She looked around at the festivities, a warm smile lighting up her face as she took in the over-the-top decorations. "Everything looks great. You guys outdid yourselves."

"We went a little overboard on the red, white and blue theme, but it's only once a year, right? We're allowed," he said with a chuckle.

"Of course," Ava answered with a grin. "Who doesn't need a life-sized cutout of Uncle Sam at their Fourth of July party? Not to mention I saw a few people with blue paint on their faces when I walked in." She gave him a thumbs-up. "You coast guard folks sure know how to be patriotic."

Ava was greeted warmly by the members of his team. While Bridget was talking to Ava, Paddy ambled over to him, a huge smile overtaking his face. At sixty years old, he was the most senior member of his team and affectionately known as the heart and soul of it. With graying temples and a mustache and beard, he had an air of distinction. Sawyer couldn't count how many times over the years he'd served as his sounding board.

"Something you want to tell us?" Paddy wagged his eyebrows in Ava's direction.

He shook his head and smiled. "Is it that obvious?"

"Only to someone who really knows you." He clapped Sawyer on the shoulder. "You look mighty good together."

"We're not together, Paddy," he explained. "Not like that. Not yet, anyway." He was fumbling with his words, not sure how to explain something even he didn't fully understand.

"What's holding you back?" Paddy asked. "Is it Billy?"

He shrugged, not wanting to get into a long explanation of all the whys and wherefores. "There's a lot of reasons we shouldn't even consider being together. I'm not so sure we can get past all our obstacles."

"And yet here the two of you are, together." Paddy glanced over at Ava, then back at Sawyer. "I can't decide which one of you has the bigger smile plastered on your face. Sometimes we worry too much about how things might look or what others might say instead of focusing on how we feel."

Sawyer grimaced. "It's not that simple. There are things I should have told her a long time ago, but I didn't. And now, after all this time, I don't know how to broach it. At first, I thought I'd be bringing her more pain by unloading on her. Now I'm wondering if this whole time I've just been scared. The very idea of telling her knocks the wind out of me."

"It's never too late to make things right." Paddy reached out and grasped Sawyer by the shoulders, his blue eyes steely as he looked him straight in the eye. "And in regards to being scared, it happens to the best of us. Don't let it stop you from going after what you want."

All of a sudden Ava walked up, her face lit up with a lighthearted grin. "I hope I'm not interrupting," she said with a glance in Paddy's direction, "but I've been waiting for Sawyer to ask me to dance ever since I got here. I guess I'm just going to have to ask him instead." She held out her hand and smiled at him, reeling him in without having to utter a single word.

"I'd love to," he blurted out. Both Paddy and Ava laughed at his eagerness. As he slipped his hand in hers and led Ava to the makeshift dance floor, he let all of his doubts drift away. Just for this one moment in time he would suspend reality and pretend as if all was right with the world. As Ava settled into his arms and they began swaying to the music, he found himself wishing this night would never end.

Ava couldn't remember the last time she'd enjoyed herself so much on the Fourth of July. She didn't feel out of place or awkward in the slightest. That had been a big fear of hers, and the reason she'd almost refused Sawyer's invitation. Two years was a long time to be out of the loop. The guests were a cross section of coast guard employees, folks they'd gone to school with and members of the congregation. Looking around her, Ava realized she knew almost everybody here. The members of Sawyer's team were treating her like a queen.

Several of her former clients had warmly approached

her, and she'd been gratified to tell them she was planning to open her business. Graciously, they'd promised to help her get the word out. On the spur of the moment she came up with the idea of having a relaunch party at the end of the summer. It would be a great way to create some buzz about her company. She felt a sudden burst of enthusiasm as she envisioned working with new clients and creating memorable events. Excitement was building inside her, stoked by the idea that her new business would soon be a reality. Sawyer had gone to replenish the ice supply and fill up the soda chest. She was standing a little off to the side, staring out over the dimly lit beach. There were a few partygoers who'd been brave enough to venture out into the water. High-pitched laughter rent the air as their bodies hit the cold ocean. The very idea of swimming in the frigid ocean made her shiver. "Don't tell me you're tempted to join them." She looked up to find Colby standing next to her, a teasing smile on his face. He was a friendly guy who she'd always enjoyed being around because of his warm and easygoing nature.

She raised an eyebrow at him. "I may be a Cape Cod girl, born and bred, but there's nothing that could convince me to get into that water."

He laughed good-naturedly. "I'm glad you could make it, Ava. It means a lot to Sawyer to have you here."

"I'm happy to be here. Sawyer was so excited about it, I had to come and see what all the fuss was about."

"Well, he is the guest of honor, in a sense. Everyone couldn't wait to celebrate his homecoming. People came all the way from Duxbury for this event."

"That's great, Colby. I know what his coast guard buddies mean to him. You're like family."

Colby grinned and nodded in agreement. "It's great to have him stateside, isn't it? Especially since we almost lost him."

Ava froze as the words settled in around her. "Lost him? What are you talking about?"

Colby's face blanched. He started tripping all over himself, getting tangled up in his own words. "I—I… shouldn't have mentioned it. Please, forget I said anything. It's nothing."

"Colby. Tell me! What is it?" She didn't like the strident sound of her voice, but she couldn't help it. She was alarmed. The distraught look on Colby's face spoke volumes.

His shoulders slumped and his body sagged a little. He raked his hand through his hair, letting out an agonized groan as he did so. "I shouldn't have said anything. When Sawyer was in Sierra Leone he contracted cholera. I didn't find out about it until weeks afterward. His parents don't even know." Colby's expression was somber. "He was sick, Ava. Gravely ill. There was a point when the doctors didn't think he would make it."

Although she'd wanted the truth from Colby, she hadn't expected to receive such startling news. Sawyer had been at death's door in Africa and not a soul had known about it. Not his family or his team members. Not Pastor Felix. Not her. A feeling of panic slid through her like a snake, twisting her insides so she could barely breathe. She'd almost lost him! He'd been on the other side of the world in a foreign land trying to do good for the world. And he'd nearly lost his life in doing so. *Just like Billy.* She clutched her stomach, feeling sick at the notion that Sawyer had been so close to death and she hadn't felt it. Why hadn't she sensed it? He was like a part of her, embedded so deeply into her essence she'd always assumed she would know if he was in harm's way.

Colby reached out and gently grabbed her by the hands. "Ava, it's all right. Sawyer is fine. He's healthy... and happy. He's home."

His voice was soothing and sure, but she still felt fear rising in her throat. It was choking her, and she found it difficult to breathe.

"But he almost died," she gasped. "He could have—"

"That's in the past. Right here, right now, he's fine," Colby said in a calm tone.

"I can't—" she said through shallow breaths "—can't talk about this. Not now." She pushed her way past Colby, past a group of revelers and down the board-walk toward the water's edge.

"Please, God. Help me," she panted as she struggled to breathe. She knew what was happening to her. It had happened several times before when she'd felt overwhelmed with anxiety. Her chest was tight and she was gasping for air. It felt as if everything was crashing down around her. She was having a panic attack.

Learning about Sawyer's brush with death had been too much for her mind to absorb. Losing him was just too terrifying of a concept. A flood of memories from that fateful night came crashing back to her. The long, endless hours of waiting by the phone. The kids peppering her with questions about their father's whereabouts. Being told his cold, lifeless body had been taken to the morgue. The rush of feelings she'd battled—fear and pain and regret. And an overwhelming sadness. She knelt down in the sand. As she willed herself to take deep, even breaths she heard someone calling her name. A low voice whispered reassurances in her ear as strong arms encircled her. The smell of sandalwood hovered in the air. A gentle hand touched her face. Without a doubt she knew she was being held in Sawyer's comforting embrace.

"Try to breathe, Ava. You can do it. Come on." Over and over again he repeated the words as he watched her struggle to calm herself. He'd witnessed her mad dash across the beach, and he'd headed Colby off at the pass as he followed after her. Taking matters into his own hands, he'd run after her down by the water, concerned by her jerky body movements and sudden departure from the festivities.

It was painful to see her like this. She was on her knees in the sand. Her skin had paled and her eyes were wide with panic. Her breathing was erratic and choppy. He began massaging her back between her shoulder blades, trying to comfort her in any way he could. He'd seen panic attacks before, and he was fairly certain Ava was experiencing one. Although her life wasn't in jeopardy, he knew people felt as if they were dying while they were in the midst of one. Words of comfort flowed from his mouth like quicksilver and he saw her gradually calming herself. He watched as she sucked in air. Her breathing was slowing down and returning to normal. Her chest wasn't heaving as dramatically as it had been.

She took a deep breath. "Thanks. I feel like such an idiot," she said in a shaky voice. "When did I become so weak?"

"You're not an idiot. And you're one of the strongest people I've ever known." He ran his hands up and down her arms in a soothing gesture. "It seemed like you were having a panic attack. Has this happened before?"

"A few times," she admitted, her face reddening. "Never quite as bad as this one. That was scary."

He frowned at Ava, not quite understanding what had transpired while he was gone. "You were fine when I left you to get the sodas. What happened?"

Her jaw trembled, and she studied him with a wary expression. "Sometimes I get anxious about things.... It happens when I feel overwhelmed."

She hesitated, biting her lip and looking up at him with her soft hazel eyes. "Please don't be mad at Colby. He slipped and told me you were near death in Africa."

Her eyes welled up and she squeezed them shut. She swiped away the moisture from her cheeks. "I'm so sorry you went through it all alone."

He clenched down on his teeth as he battled against a rising tide of anger. "Colby should have kept his mouth shut. It wasn't his story to tell. Not to mention he's upset you."

"His heart was in the right place. He was telling me how happy he is you're back in town. He made a comment about almost losing you, and I kept pressing him about it."

Sawyer groaned. "I didn't want anyone to worry about me. Not you. Or my parents. Or Daniel." He grimaced. "After everything this family has been through in the past few years…I didn't want to lay this at your feet."

"There are some things you can't protect us from. It's called life." She reached out and grazed her fingers across his forehead. "You've got an angry look in your eye, Sawyer Trask. And this furrow in your brow…I don't like it. It means you're holding on to anger. Take it from me. You don't want to do that."

"No, I don't want that. For either one of us. I don't ever want to be consumed by such a negative emotion." On impulse, he reached out and caressed her cheek. Her eyes widened, and she was gazing up at him with such a look of longing. It mirrored everything he was feeling for her, all the emotions he'd kept bottled up inside. He dipped his head down and captured her lips in a tender, emotional kiss. As he brushed his lips over hers, he felt hope flare within him. After so many years of running away from his feelings, it felt nice to wear his heart on his sleeve. Ava leaned into the kiss, her lips sweet and warm against his.

He swept his fingers down the graceful slope of her neck, making his touch as light as a feather. As the kiss ended Ava let out a soft sigh. As they drew apart, their gazes locked, and he noticed her eyes glistening. Her face was slightly flushed. With the moonlight as her backdrop, she was simply beautiful.

"You're not going to disappear now, are you?" Her voice held a hint of mischief.

He felt a huge grin cross his face. "You can't get rid of me that easily."

She began fiddling with her fingers. He could see the telltale signs of worry on her face—the tiny crease on her brow and the wariness in her eyes.

"I'm not going anywhere. Really. Truly." He softened his voice, wanting it to sound like a caress. "I'm at my best when I'm home in Buzzards Bay."

"That's good," she said with a shy grin. "Because I kind of like having you around. And the thought of something bad happening to you…of nearly losing you—it hurts." His heart pinged inside his chest. It was the first time Ava had put her feelings into words. Although he'd felt something shifting between them, experience had taught him not to dream of anything more than friendship. But this kiss, this tender moment, held the promise of a new day.

Despite his uncle's opposition and his own reservations, he wanted to be with Ava. He wanted to hold her hand and take her for picnics in the park. He wanted to sit on the beach with her and watch the sunrise as it crept over the horizon. There were so many possibilities they could explore together.

Being without her was no longer an option.

And as fireworks lit up the obsidian sky, he reached out and clasped Ava's hand, buoyed by the way she squeezed his own in return. The way she was smiling at him, that tender, enraptured look on her face, made him feel ten feet tall.

They stood side by side, arms touching, hands joined together. The weight of the moment had them both enthralled. There was only one thing standing in the way of it being sheer perfection. Somehow he needed to find a way to tell Ava the truth about the night Billy died, because the longer he waited, the bigger the risk he faced of losing her forever.

Chapter Eleven

The following morning Ava found herself replaying the events of the previous evening over and over again in her mind.

Finding out about Sawyer's brush with death in Africa had been a shock. At least now she understood what he'd been trying to tell her the other day at the fair. He'd wanted to come clean with her about nearly dying from cholera.

Despite her panic attack and the news about Sawyer, she'd had an enjoyable time at the party. Dancing. Fireworks. Friends. That fantastic kiss! Just the thought of it caused her lips to tingle, and she lightly brushed her fingertips against them. If she closed her eyes it would be easy to transport herself back to that moment when they'd kissed on the beach.

"Get your head out of the clouds," she murmured, willing herself to stop thinking about Sawyer. It was a task easier said than done, considering she had a clear view of his lighthouse from where she was standing on the lawn. So far it was shaping up to be a hot and hazy Cape Cod day. The forecast was calling for blue skies, with the July temperature rising into the mid-eighties by noontime. At the moment she was trying to wrangle a frisky puppy into a pail of suds. It was high time Tully had himself a proper bath, she'd decided. Casey and Dolly were supposed to be helping her, but they'd bailed the moment they spotted Sawyer walking down on the beach. "Tully! Behave yourself," she muttered. Tully was wiggling around in the bucket, sloshing the water over the sides in his attempt to break free. She let out a groan as the dirty water splashed onto her white cotton shirt. Determined to finish the job, she held the puppy with one hand while she lathered him up with the other. She then turned the hose on him, gently spraying him with warm water. A few minutes later she was toweling him dry, marveling at how nice he smelled.

"Aren't you the pretty boy?" she cooed as Tully shot her a miffed look. He then shook his body with all his might, water flying in her direction. She let out a surprised cry, sending Tully scampering off into the house. Loud, high-pitched cries heralded the arrival of the twins, who raced toward her at full speed. They were practically stumbling over each other in an effort to be the first one to reach her side.

"Mom! Mom! Sawyer wants to take us out on the water. Can we?" Casey asked.

"He says we can ride around the harbor," Dolly added. "Please say yes."

"Not today," she answered in a brisk tone. *Not any day,* she really wanted to say. She busied herself by picking up the pail of dirty water and overturning it into a bed of mulch. When she was finished she wiped her hands on her shorts and walked inside the house.

The twins trailed behind her, their voices intermingled as they continued to beg her to go out on Sawyer's boat. Abruptly, she turned toward them, her voice sharp as she said, "No means no, guys. I've heard what you had to say and I've given you an answer."

All of sudden Sawyer was standing in her kitchen, his brow furrowed as he looked back and forth between her and the children. "What's going on?"

"She said we can't go out on your boat," Casey wailed. His eyes were beginning to tear up.

"That's the same thing she says when Doug wants to take us out on his fishing boat," Dolly said in a defiant tone. "It's always a big fat no."

"It's not a long trip, if that makes any difference," Sawyer explained. "Just to Woods Hole and back. Shouldn't be more than a couple hours."

"No!" she cried out. "I don't want them out on the water. It's not safe."

Panic seized her at the thought of her babies being out at sea. They were so little and defenseless. If something were to go wrong with the boat, how would they manage to survive?

"They'll be fine with me, Ava," Sawyer responded in an even tone. "The water is as smooth as glass today. There's nothing to worry about. I promise not to take my eyes off them."

Ava bristled. She knew he was trying to pacify her, and it only served to annoy her more. They were her children! She was a single mother now, and it was her job to keep them safe. Protected from unsafe waters and leaky boats. Safe from choppy seas and unexpected squalls.

"Please, Mom. Can we?" Casey begged. "Uncle Sawyer will keep us safe."

"I said no," she repeated, her heart sinking at the defeated look in the twins' eyes. On some level she knew that she was being irrational, but she couldn't help it. Billy had drowned out on that water, and as much as she loved the ocean, she didn't trust it. It was unthinkable that she would send her precious children out on the very waters where their father had died. She doubted that she ever would.

"Kids, go to your room." Her tone was clipped and no-nonsense.

"But Mom," Dolly whined. "Why can't we stay here?"

All Ava had to do was shoot a look at Dolly, letting her know she wasn't entertaining any arguments. The children scooted out of the room like two frightened rabbits. As soon as they were alone, Ava turned toward Sawyer. She could feel her legs shaking and a muscle twitching by her eye. She gritted her teeth and slowly counted to three. "There are certain things that are nonnegotiable. Taking the kids out on the water—that's one of them."

Her body was trembling with rage. She was in full mama-bear mode. The very idea of the kids going out to sea made her feel threatened. Hostile. Under attack.

Sawyer's expression softened. "Ava, I'm sorry if I've

made you feel disrespected. That wasn't my intention. What happened to Billy isn't going to happy to Casey and Dolly. It was a perfect storm of events that night. Impossible to predict and highly unlikely to ever happen again to anyone you know." The rich, soothing timbre of his voice rang with conviction. But her fears were too deep-rooted to be swayed by Sawyer's calm and reason.

She could already feel the panic setting in. Her chest felt tight. Her hands were clammy. Pretty soon her breathing was going to become ragged. Just the thought of that awful night—Billy not coming home, the call from the coast guard, learning from Sawyer that he'd identified him at the morgue. The one memory she'd blocked from her mind was the moment when she'd gathered the twins together to tell them about their father's death. It had been nightmarish. And she never allowed herself to go to that dark place, that soul-stripping moment. Just the thought of it made her break out in a cold sweat. She held up her hand to stop him from talking.

"Stop trying to placate me. You have no idea how I feel, how frightening this is for me. How could you?"

A look of pain crossed his face. "I'm sorry for pushing. You know I'd never hurt you. And you're right. In a million years I could never know how it feels to bury the person I love."

"I lost Billy. I can't lose the twins." Her voice cracked as she confided her deepest, darkest fear. Ever since Billy's death she'd been racked with fear over the possibility of losing Dolly and Casey. She felt moisture on her cheeks. "I won't be responsible for another person's death." Her voice rang out stronger than she felt at the moment. It was her own private guilt and shame that she'd driven Billy out of the house the night he died.

Sawyer shook his head, confusion written all over his face. "What are you talking about, Ava?"

She hung her head, not wanting to see the look in his eyes when she told him the truth. Not a single soul other than her two sisters knew about the blistering argument she'd had with Billy the night he'd died. No one knew what a colossal failure she'd been as a wife.

"I blame myself for Billy's death! If we hadn't gotten into an argument that night, he wouldn't have taken off the way he did. Whenever we fought that's what he did. He would storm out of the house and head to the nearest bar or liquor store so he could drink. I knew that! I knew he didn't like to be pushed into a corner. Don't you get it? It's my fault."

He rushed toward her, pulling her into his arms without hesitation. At first she fought it, keeping her body ramrod straight. She lost all of her fight, burrowing into the warmth of Sawyer's embrace. She let out a shudder and sobbed. It felt so good to be held by him, to be sheltered by strong, nurturing arms. For the first time in a long while she felt protected. Safe. And it had everything to do with the fact that it was Sawyer who was holding her.

"Shh, Ava. Shh," he crooned as he rubbed her back in a comforting gesture. "Don't ever say that. What would make you even think that? You were the most loving, giving wife to Billy. There wasn't anything you wouldn't have done for him."

She pulled away from him, looking up at him so that she could look him in the eye. Sawyer's eyes truly were the mirrors of his soul. There wasn't anything he could hide once you looked in his eyes. It had always been that way with him. And she desperately wanted to see the truth there. "I wasn't a good wife."

"What?" Sawyer asked. His tone was sharp. He had a floored expression on his face. "Where is all this coming from?"

"I didn't get him the help he needed." She let out a harsh laugh. "Oh, I made threats. I made him sleep in the guest room. I even threatened to leave him a few times. But in the end, he always managed to charm his way out of it." Tears were falling fast and furiously now, and she swiped them away, angry at herself for falling apart.

Sawyer frowned. His eyes darkened and his mouth was set in a firm line. "Billy had a serious problem. You can't assume the blame for that. What about all the times he promised he'd get help? What about all the centers you looked into for him to get treatment?"

"No! Don't say that—" she began. "I can't go down that road, Sawyer. Please." Her voice was shaky and her limbs had a bad case of tremors. "I'm sorry about the boat outing. I wish I was ready to let them go, but I'm not."

Heat rose to her cheeks. She was mortified by her outburst. Two years later and she was still terrified by the idea of going out on the water. Having spent her childhood on sailboats, traveling on ferries to the Vineyard and enjoying leisurely excursions on her family's boat, it was particularly painful to be in such limbo. Loving the ocean, yet terrified of its raw power. Sawyer reached out and placed his hands on her shoulders, his touch gentle and grounding. All she wanted to do was burrow herself into his chest and find refuge from all her fears. Once again she'd let fear take over, and in the process denied her kids an outing.

"You don't have to apologize. It's my fault. I wasn't thinking, Ava. I had no idea this was still an issue."

"The thought of something happening to them frightens me." Somehow she felt the need to explain what had just happened. "I know it's not rational, but the idea of them being out on the water makes me break out into a cold sweat."

"Of course it's terrifying. It brings up some of the darkest moments of your life. I should have been more sensitive to that." His voice broke. "Forgive me."

She let out a shaky laugh. "Forgive you? You've done nothing wrong. Even now, you're trying to do something nice for my children." Her gaze settled on Sawyer's strong, handsome face. He looked so wounded. His expression was so somber it caused her heart to painfully contract. She felt such tenderness toward him. Sweet, wonderful Sawyer.

She reached up and brushed a kiss across his cheekbone. Her eyes locked with his, she said, "And for the record, Sawyer, I could forgive you almost anything."

* * *

"I wasn't a good wife. I could forgive you almost anything." The words rocketed through him like an explosion. An hour after he'd left Ava, he was still grappling with the aftershocks. He'd wanted to tell her everything in that very moment, but with the twins in the house he'd known it wasn't the right time or place. It wouldn't be fair to unload everything on Ava with the kids in the house to witness it. He wouldn't hurt Casey or Dolly for the world. Or Ava.

He'd seen it all in her eyes. And it had nearly gutted him. The guilt and the pain. The nagging doubts. When she'd voiced her pain about having not being a good wife, he'd felt as if all the air had been pushed out of his lungs. It killed him to see her judge herself so harshly. He couldn't bear to hear her take the blame for all of Billy's failings. Perhaps if he'd come clean two years ago about his fight with Billy, she wouldn't be blaming herself. Maybe then she'd have shifted the blame squarely on his shoulders and off her own. But he hadn't known. He'd had no clue she'd been holding herself responsible. He was still having trouble wrapping his head around the fact. The irony was shocking. They were both holding themselves accountable for his death.

There was no way to go back and undo the decisions he'd made. At this point he had no other choice but to act. Even though he'd always rejected the hero label, the title had still been attached to his name. Sawyer Trask. Hero. Like it or not, it was part of his identity. It wasn't heroic to allow Ava to spend another minute of her life wondering about Billy's last hours. It wasn't noble to let her continue to beat herself up over fault. Blame. Guilt.

Last night he'd tossed and turned for hours, replaying the conversation with her over and over again in his head. And despite the fact that he'd made peace with his cousin's death, he needed to see Ava through that process. He wouldn't rest until she was fully healed. And if getting answers about the night Billy died provided closure, then it was a no-brainer. There wasn't a single doubt in his mind of what he needed to do, even though it might prove to be one of the hardest conversations of his life.

As the sun crested over the horizon, a fiery burst of color against a backdrop of pink and purple sky, Sawyer stood on the parapet and greeted the dawn like an old friend. Ava merited love and devotion and honesty. She deserved to be with someone who would put her above everything else. In the deepest regions of his heart, he believed those thing would heal her heart. More than he'd ever wanted anything in his life, he wanted to be the person to give her all those wonderful things. There was so much at stake—her happiness, her future, the children's well-being. The time had come to tell the truth, because the way he felt about her left him no other choice. Ava deserved the very best things in life, and he wanted to be the one to give them to her. *Please, God,* he prayed, *let this road I'm traveling be a path toward new beginnings.*

Ava sat at her kitchen table, up to her elbows in papers, pencils and folders. Her computer sat next to her, the screen displaying a lovely beach landscape with her name written across the top. Since she was totally revamping her business plan, she'd decided to come up with a new name, as well. Occasions. It was simple yet elegant. Hopefully it would tell potential clients something about her outlook on life. Despite the personal setbacks she'd suffered over the past few years, she still believed in celebrating life's grand occasions with family and friends. Memories could be cherished for a lifetime.

Last night Sawyer had been so encouraging about her reestablishing her party business, it had lit a fire within her. His belief in her made her think she could climb mountains. For the past two hours she'd been ordering business cards, creating a new website and brainstorming ideas. Instead of paying rent for an office in town, she could transform the small, spare bedroom upstairs into a workspace. And to create a little buzz, she could host a relaunch party. Excitement pulsed in the air as ideas came to her fast and furiously.

She had Sawyer to thank for getting her energized and hopeful. His return from Africa had been her catalyst for change. So much had changed since his return. It seemed that no matter how long they'd gone without speaking, they were able to pick up where they'd left off. They connected. She'd told him things about her life with Billy she'd never divulged to a single soul. And he'd listened to every word, serving as the sounding board she so needed.

The kids were spending the morning at the aquarium with their grandparents. Although she liked having some time to herself, the house took on a different quality without the kids bustling around. At times the silence was deafening. She was accustomed to little voices constantly chattering, whether it was a lively conversation or a sibling squabble. A sudden knock at the back door provided a welcome distraction from the solitude.

She opened the door to find Sawyer standing there, looking casual in a pair of jeans and a T-shirt. "Hey. Good morning. I didn't expect to see you so bright and early." Her voice registered her surprise. She held up her mug of coffee. "Would you like some? I just brewed a pot."

He held up a hand. "No, I'm good. Ava, there's something we need to talk about. I would have done this last night, but with Dolly and Casey home—"

"Uh-oh. What have the twins been up to now?" Her tone was teasing, designed to make Sawyer smile. She loved his joyful spirit and the way the lines around his mouth creased whenever he grinned. The somber look on his face caused a trickle of panic to skitter along her spine.

He grimaced. "I wish this was as simple as that."

She reached out and laced her hands through his as a gesture of comfort and solidarity. Whatever was going on, they could deal with it together. She was going to support him now as he'd always supported her.

"What is it? You're scaring me." She could hear the thudding of her heart.

"It was tough last night hearing you blame yourself for Billy's death. For weeks now I've been trying to find a way to tell you something I should have told you a long time ago." She watched as he shoved his hands into his pockets and rocked back on his heels.

"I need to tell you about the night Billy died."

Chapter Twelve

"Sawyer, what is this all about?" Her brain felt fuzzy. Somehow she felt as if she wasn't connecting the dots. He looked so grim and serious, as if the world as he knew it was coming to an end. "What do you need to tell me?"

"The night Billy died, he came by the shop and we got into it." His tone was clipped. There was no hint of his usual warm and fuzzy vibe. His eyes were wide and a tremor danced along his jaw.

All she could do was repeat his words back to him. "Got into it?"

"We had a pretty bad argument." The words reverberated in her ears.

"I didn't know that. Why—why didn't I know that?" A puzzled feeling swept over her. "Wh-what did you fight about?"

"He was supposed to come by the shop that morning. By the time he showed up, it was dark outside. I was upset with him because he'd been shirking his duties for weeks. He'd been drinking, Ava. I could smell it on his breath. You know how Billy could be sometimes. He said some things about my wanting to be your husband. Crazy stuff."

The words coming out of his mouth packed quite a punch.

"What? Why—why would he have said that? That doesn't make any sense." Ava's mouth felt dry and her hands were trembling. Her limbs felt like rubber bands.

Sawyer's gaze remained locked on hers, but he stayed silent. A thick tension hung in the air.

"What did you say to him?"

"I told him he was out of line." The creases around his mouth were born of tension and strain. He didn't look like himself. Instinctively, she knew there was more he wasn't saying. She'd known Sawyer for too long and too well not to see the telltale signs. There was something he was holding back. And she knew it wasn't good.

Without hesitation she advanced toward him, her movements full of purpose. They were now standing so close they could feel each other's breath on their faces. "Is that all?" she pressed him. "Tell me. I need to know."

A muscle twitched by the corner of his mouth. "I told him he was right," he admitted. "I told him I'd thought of being your husband, that he hadn't been treating you and the kids as he should have…that I would have treated you better."

Suddenly her legs felt as if they might give out on her. They felt as rubbery as hot noodles. Her hand reached out to grab the kitchen counter. If not for that, she might have lost her balance.

"You had no right to say those things!" she spit out.

"He was my cousin, Ava. We'd butted heads many times before. I know it sounds bad, but we were used to being open and honest with each other. I had no way of knowing—"

"No! No! My husband went out on the water because of that argument. It's what he always did when he was upset. You know that! And he was legally drunk at the time of the accident—that's what the autopsy stated."

Although part of her felt a stab of sympathy for the ravaged look on his face, another part of her wanted to lash out at him.

"He was an alcoholic. He didn't drink because of our argument. Or because of you. Or losing his job or the pressure. They may have added some strain, but he drank because he couldn't not drink."

He stroked his chin with his hand. His eyes were stormy with emotion. "And he didn't get in that boat because of me. It's taken me a long time to come to terms with that, but as a father and a husband, Billy made choices that night. That doesn't make him a bad person…he had a disease, Ava. It simply made him human."

She raised her finger and stabbed it in his direction. "You…stop it!" she growled. "You have no right to say these things about him. Don't try to paint him as this…sick, damaged person. He was a good father and he loved us. He loved me." The tears were flowing freely now and she didn't bother to wipe them away.

She was in so much pain and feeling very vulnerable. How could Sawyer be saying these terrible things to her about Billy? Didn't he know he was putting a dagger in her heart?

Sawyer let out a groan. "Billy was an amazing person. From the time we were little he was my own personal hero. My older cousin who could do everything better and faster. There was nothing Billy couldn't do as far as I was concerned. He was everything to me." He let out a ragged breath. "I know how much he loved you. He wore it on his sleeve every day of his life. I'm not trying to take anything away from you, from what you shared. You and the kids were his world." He reached out and placed his hands on her shoulders, looking deeply into her eyes. His own looked wounded and turbulent. Raw pain was etched on his face.

"But Billy had problems long before the two of you ever started dating. He had DUIs in college and he was arrested for drunk and disorderly."

She winced as he listed Billy's transgressions. The words were going round and round in her head like a merry-go-round. All she wanted was for him to stop talking so she could find a quiet corner and think. What she really needed was a few minutes to catch her breath.

"I'm not trying to slam him. Don't you see what I'm trying to say? This wasn't about you or me or his family. It was about his illness."

She pushed his hands away from her, using more force than was necessary. "This conversation feels so disloyal to Billy. He's not here to defend himself. That's so unfair to him." She took a deep breath and stood up straight. Despite the hurt, she could handle this. She was strong, she reminded herself. She'd endured way worse than this betrayal. "I'd like you to leave, Sawyer."

"This doesn't change anything between us. What we feel. What we've been building toward." Sawyer's voice was gentle and soothing. He reached out and brushed his knuckles against her cheek, his touch as light as a feather. She steeled herself against how good his touch felt, knowing Sawyer had crossed a line with her that couldn't be undone. It was confusing to be so angry at him, yet still want to be soothed by his tender touch.

"You're just scared. Frightened by what you're feeling. Terrified of loving another person who might leave you. But I'm not going anywhere. Never again."

His words were filled with so much comfort and the promise of brighter days. She wanted to forgive him his lie of omission. Part of her ached to run toward him and find shelter in the comfort of his healing embrace. But she couldn't. Because at this moment she felt as if she were still Billy's wife, still tied to him like an anchor. Who was she if she wasn't Mrs. Billy Trask? What would it say about her if she moved on to another man? Billy's cousin, no less. Her feelings for Sawyer made her feel guilty, unfaithful. Even though Billy had died, she was still his wife, wasn't she? The mother of his children?

"Please leave," she begged. There were too many confusing thoughts running around in her head. She didn't know what to think or feel. She was beginning to feel numb. Hot tears streamed down her face. She swiped them away as a cold anger swept through her.

"Please don't ask me to leave. Let's just talk this out. I wasn't trying to hide this from you. Don't you see, Ava? I was dealing with my own grief, my own shame. For a long time I've been blaming myself, just like you. What I really believe is that these feelings of guilt are tied up in loss and grief."

"I don't want to hear any more of this! Go! Now! Before the children come back home," she pleaded. "I can't even bear to look at you right now!" Her voice rang out sharp and strident in the stillness of the kitchen.

"I'll go," he answered in a quiet voice. "But first you need to know something. I made a promise to Billy about looking after Casey and Dolly. I intend to keep that promise."

Ava put her face in her hands and began sobbing. Despite her vow to be strong, she felt as if she'd plunged back into mourning. Her faith in Sawyer had been absolute. Now it was shattered. Irreparable damage had been done to their relationship. Yet again, she had to deal with a staggering loss. Seconds later she heard the back door close with a firm click, and she knew Sawyer had honored her wishes. He was gone. Instead of feeling happy that he'd left, she felt numb.

She sagged against the kitchen counter, feeling as if all the life had been drained out of her. A feeling of sorrow swept over her, and she struggled to hold it together. The kids would be returning from their outing soon, and the last thing she wanted them to witness was their mother falling apart. They'd already seen too much of it in the past few years. Their lives should be filled with joy and exploration, not sadness and uncertainty.

She looked around at her empty house. There was such a void now that Sawyer was gone, as well as an ache in her heart that time wouldn't be able to heal. His positive energy had always infused her house with light and warmth and love. He was embedded in her heart right along with all her childhood memories. Just as she was beginning to believe in second chances, life had stepped in and given her a reality check. There wouldn't be any happy ending for her and Sawyer. The chasm between them was too wide to cross, and the trust she'd placed in him had been fractured beyond repair.

Sawyer had barely slept a wink last night. He'd tossed and turned for hours, replaying over and over again in his mind the events of earlier that day. It had taken every ounce of his will to make himself leave Ava's cottage. He'd wanted to stay and plead his case, to convince her of his sincere regret. But he knew she wasn't ready to hear anything he had to say. She was stuck. Entrenched in her belief that someone was responsible for Billy's death, she'd chosen to place the blame at his feet. And even though it stung bitterly to have Ava think so poorly of him, a part of him understood. Two years after Billy's death she was still trying to make logical sense out of a senseless tragedy. Somehow, Ava believed if she could put the pieces of the puzzle together it would all make sense. She hadn't figured out yet that there were some things in life without explanation.

Sharp, savage pain speared through him as he remembered all the harsh words she'd thrown at him. It flooded over him in unrelenting waves. Seeing Ava in that terrible state had been agonizing. She'd looked at him as if he were a monster. As if she didn't know him at all. That's what hurt the most. It was as if everything that had come before now ceased to exist. Their past—their lifelong friendship—was in tatters.

As it was, he was barely holding up, wanting nothing more than to hide away and lick his wounds in private. And he was wounded. Badly. He felt as if he'd been run over by a truck. All day he'd been going through the motions—a full day at work, a few errands and now this quick stop at his parents' house. They'd asked him to swing by and take a look at their outdoor grill that had been giving them problems. When he arrived at their house he'd instantly spotted Uncle Troy's car parked in the driveway. The foursome was having a cookout tonight and enjoying a lazy summer evening. It was amazing how life could go on as usual when he was so torn up inside.

He just wanted to get in and fix the grill, then get out as quickly as possible. After greeting everyone he made his way outside to the patio and began tinkering with the grill. In a matter of minutes he'd solved the problem.

"Cookout crisis averted," he muttered as he turned on the burner and saw flames come roaring to life. The sound of footsteps hitting the stone patio echoed in the silence. He turned around, coming face-to-face with his uncle. A brief tension hung in the air as they eyeballed each other. It didn't take a genius to figure out something was up.

Finally, Uncle Troy spoke. "I owe you an apology, son."

Sawyer studied Uncle Troy without uttering a single word. He didn't have a clue what he was talking about, nor was he really in the mood for guessing games. His heart was bruised and battered. Everything was a little out of focus at the moment. Although he loved and respected his uncle, nothing could be as earth-shattering as what had happened between him and Ava. Not a single thing could be as important.

"I had no right to say those things to you last year." He cleared his throat. "About you and Ava. I was out of line for telling you to stay away from her." He scratched his bald head. "It's pretty clear to me it was one of the reasons you left for Sierra Leone. I've felt very guilty about that."

Sawyer shrugged. "It's all right. I understood. She's your daughter-in-law. You thought I was crossing a line with her."

His uncle grimaced. "No, Sawyer. I know you better than that. You're the last person who would ever do that. You've always been upstanding and fine. All along, it's been my problem. Nancy only objected to the relationship because she didn't want to see me hurt. Somehow I thought that keeping the two of you apart was protecting Billy." He sniffled as tears misted in his eyes. Sawyer couldn't remember ever having seen his uncle so emotional. "You see, I could never protect him while he was alive. The illness he had…there was nothing we could do to help him, try as we might."

"I know how much you loved him. How much you

still love him. And I know what his loss means to you and Aunt Nancy. Losing your only child…" Sawyer's voice got husky and trailed off.

Uncle Troy nodded in agreement. "Yep, I miss him like crazy. Nothing can fill that hole. And I know you feel the same sense of loss, Sawyer. The two of you were real close."

"I think about him every day." He'd miss his cousin for the rest of his life. Of that he was certain. Even though their relationship hadn't been perfect, there had been real love between them.

"Life is short. Sometimes happiness is fleeting. If I've learned anything at all from my son's death it's to not leave anything unsaid. Whatever you feel for Ava, don't let another day go by without telling her what's on your heart. Leave it all on the table, son."

"I appreciate you saying this, but Ava and I… It's not going to happen for us. There's too much standing between us." He struggled to speak past the lump in his throat. It meant so much to him that his uncle was giving him his blessing, but it was a moot point. Ava wanted nothing to do with him. And there was an unrelenting ache in his heart that reached all the way down to his soul.

"Do you love her?"

"Yes, I do. A part of me always has, ever since we were kids," he acknowledged. "But I never acted on it. I would never have disrespected her marriage like that."

"You're preaching to the choir, Sawyer. I know what an incredible man you are. You've always put others above yourself, both in your personal life and in your profession. Your moral compass is pure gold."

"Truth is, since I've been back from overseas I've managed to fall completely head over heels in love with her. I've never felt anything like this in my entire life." He was still in awe over the feelings Ava inspired.

His uncle grinned and clapped him on the back. "Have you told her?" he asked, a joyful smile lighting up his face.

He sighed, wishing it didn't hurt so much knowing he might never get the chance. "Not exactly. I haven't gotten the chance. We seem to be at odds at the moment."

He hesitated for a moment, unsure of whether or not he should tell his uncle about his fight with Billy. There was no point in keeping it a secret anymore, he realized. Withholding the truth had earned him nothing but heartache. "I told her Billy and I had a fight the night he died. Tensions were running high between us because of the business and we both said things we shouldn't have. Bottom line is she blames me for him going out on the water, for the accident, for everything...." His voice trailed off. He braced himself for Uncle Troy's reaction.

His uncle shook his head, his expression one of dismay. "Why is it that we've all been blaming ourselves for Billy's death? Why can't we just accept that it was a tragic accident, a perfect storm of events that led to unspeakable loss?"

Sawyer shrugged. For some time now he'd been wondering the same thing. "There's such a thing as survivor guilt. I've seen it in the coast guard. There have been situations in which people perish while others survive.

It sets up a scenario where the survivors feel a sense of shame or guilt because they lived."

"Your aunt and I have shouldered our share of the blame, as well. Did we indulge him too much? Not give him enough love? Should we have disciplined him more? The questions are endless. And in the end, there still aren't any solid answers. The best I can figure is that as smart Billy was, and as much as he loved his family, he just couldn't find a way to hold things together. He couldn't get that monkey off his back. And as his father, I've got to accept that."

When Troy had approached Sawyer one year ago, he'd been full of censure. It had hurt him badly, reminding him way too much of the last words he'd exchanged with Billy. Now he'd reached out to him in a humble and gracious way. Uncle Troy's sentiments were profound and deeply touching. Sawyer found himself getting choked up. It amazed him how far he'd come in the past year. Not only was he rooting for his relationship with Ava, but he'd found a way to process his son's death without looking to assign blame.

As Uncle Troy had stated, life was way too short to dwell on the past. If he had to do it all again, he would make different choices. Better ones. But he couldn't change a thing. He could only hope and pray that Ava could see it in her heart to forgive him and realize he'd made a human mistake. At least he could honestly say he'd been trying to protect her. She'd been so fragile in the days and weeks after Billy's death. He'd been so afraid of breaking her. And now he feared that he'd done that to her anyway. Shutting his eyes, he tried to block out the images of her shattered, frantic face.

What had he done? Even though it had only been thirty-two hours since he'd seen her, he missed her like crazy. He worried about her. Was she sad? Angry? Did Casey and Dolly know anything about their falling-out? He'd called her half a dozen times or more, leaving rambling messages on her answering machine. He had a feeling she was screening her calls so she wouldn't run the risk of speaking to him. Part of him didn't blame her. Sometimes a secret felt like a lie.

He honestly didn't know how much longer he could go on like this. It was tearing him up inside—the waiting, the wondering, the longing. And even though he wasn't sure he didn't deserve to be cast out of her life, he prayed to God that time would heal these wounds.

Ava sat at her desk working on her business plan for Occasions by Ava. With a groan, she tore a page from her notebook and crumpled it up into a ball. Try as she might, she couldn't concentrate. How could she work toward her future when her present was so up in the air?

On the spur of the moment, she'd stopped by the cemetery early this morning. For two years she'd avoided coming to the grave site, unable to bear the thought of seeing Billy's name engraved on the cold marble headstone. *Billy Trask. Husband. Father. Son. Forever in our hearts.* Somehow, seeing the words didn't break her.

Finally, she'd been able to talk to Billy in a way she'd never been able to while he was alive. She'd told him about her pain and fear and loneliness. Tears had flowed as she explained in detail the tidal wave of grief and the heartache. And she'd told him that although she loved him, he'd let her and the twins down. He'd given up. Once she'd gotten everything off her chest, it was as if something inside her broke free. For so long she'd been living half a life. Somewhere along the way she'd begun to realize it wasn't good enough. Ever since Sawyer came back to town, she'd been inspired to start living again. Really living, rather than going through the motions. And confronting Billy was a huge step forward. She didn't know exactly when Sawyer had worked his way into her heart and soul. Until now, all she could do was miss him with every fiber of her being. It was an actual physical ache gnawing at her. He was coming over this evening, having promised the twins last week they'd have a game night with their favorite board games. She'd left him a message asking him to still come despite the current state of their relationship.

The twins had been counting the days until tonight, and she didn't have the heart to disappoint them. It wasn't fair to make kids suffer for grown-up problems. Truthfully, she'd been relieved when he hadn't answered his phone. She still had no idea what to say to him, how to bridge the gap. A fluttery feeling came over her at the prospect of coming face-to-face with Sawyer. She was still confused. The anger had faded, so now all she felt was emptiness. Regret. Hurt. Suddenly, she no longer knew what she was supposed to feel.

All her life she'd heard her father say, "Anger is a passing storm." Rather than blow up at Sawyer, shouldn't she have listened…really listened, to what he'd been trying to tell her? Perhaps if she'd put herself in his shoes for one moment and viewed the situation without judgment, they wouldn't be at such odds.

A heavy knock on the back door drew her out of her thoughts. A quick look at the kitchen clock told her it was six o'clock. He was a little early, although the kids wouldn't mind a bit. She walked to the door and wrenched it open, steeling herself for this encounter. Instead of Sawyer, Melanie and Doug stood on her doorstep, their arms filled with board games. A wave of disappointment washed over her. Where was Sawyer?

"Hey. Come on in," she said as she ushered them inside. "What brings you guys out here?"

"Sawyer asked us to come. He was called in for a search-and-rescue. He felt badly about not being able to bring the kids the games he promised for game night, so we're here to drop them off and fill in for him."

Ava detected a slight strain on Melanie's face despite the smile on her face. "What's the search-and-rescue?" Her heart hammered inside her chest. All day she'd had an uneasy feeling, and hearing that Sawyer had been called in on his day off told her his expertise was needed in this mission. It sounded serious.

"Some teenagers stole a sailboat and went out on the water. Chris Lees and Dawson something or other. Sawyer and his team went out to find them."

Doug shook his head. "Teenagers. They think they're invincible. Let's just hope they have some sailing experience."

"They're in good hands with Sawyer and his team. It's not too bad out there, is it?" she asked, her eyes automatically shifting toward the bay window. The water looked a bit choppy, and she knew out on the open water it could be far more treacherous.

"Problem is, those swells are at least seven feet high, maybe more. Those kids are probably fighting for their lives, if not—" Doug stopped talking and she watched Melanie give him a warning look. Ava swallowed past the lump in her throat. Fighting for their lives? And now Sawyer was out there risking his life to save two local boys from certain death. Battling seven-foot swells was no small feat. He was doing what he always did— putting everyone else above himself. Just as he'd always done with her and the twins.

What have I done? she agonized. The sound of her pounding heart thrummed in her ear. Fear grabbed her by the throat and wouldn't let go. The conditions out on the water sounded dangerous. This could end tragically for two teenagers who had the rest of their lives to live out. All of a sudden she felt restless. She needed to pour her heart and soul into something. Or someone. *Sawyer.* Life was such a tenuous thing. And tomorrows were never promised. She knew what it would do to Sawyer if this rescue ended in tragedy. He would be devastated. Why hadn't she found it in her heart to forgive Sawyer? How cruel had it been to blame him for Billy's death? There were two teenagers in harm's way. She could only imagine the terror their parents must be feeling at this very moment.

The need to see Sawyer, to smooth his furrowed brow, to wrap her arms around him in a loving embrace, rose within her. She wanted to reach out and touch his face, to anchor herself to him and tell him how much he meant to her. Brave, loyal Sawyer. The longing was so strong she had to bite down on her lip so she wouldn't cry out.

Sawyer. She loved him. A part of her always had. She'd felt so guilty about falling in love with him that she'd found a way to place a wedge between them rather than face her emotions head-on. And clinging to her life with Billy had been a way of staying firmly entrenched in the past. So much time had been wasted! Well, she wasn't going to continue making that same mistake. She wasn't going to sit on the sidelines while life-and-death matters were at stake. Sawyer had always been her rock. Now it was her turn to be his anchor. He needed her support.

In the end it all boiled down to the simplest of things. The twins. Her family. Her cottage by the sea. And Sawyer, the man she loved. And even if her in-laws objected, she was going to fight tooth and nail to win their approval.

She rushed into the living room, where Melanie and Doug were playing Blokus with Casey and Dolly. "Melanie, I have to go out. Would you mind watching the kids for me until I get back?"

She looked at her quizzically. "Of course not, Ava. We'll have game night, and then I'll put in a movie."

"I might be a while," she warned. "There's a chicken casserole warming in the oven." As she zipped up her Windbreaker, Ava began praying with a vengeance. *Dear Lord, I know You and I have been at odds for some time. I know I haven't been as prayerful and devout as*

I used to be. If You're still listening, Lord, please watch over Sawyer and keep him out of harm's way. I cannot bear to lose another person I love.

And she did love him. Her feelings were so much more than friendship. Although she'd spent a lifetime running from them, those day were over. Denying her love for Sawyer would be like holding back the ocean's tides. It would be impossible. How could loving a wonderful man like Sawyer be wrong? She hadn't betrayed Billy. There was still a special place in her heart that would always be his. She'd loved and nurtured him every day of their married lives. But Sawyer—he'd imprinted himself on her very soul way back when they were kids. He was as much a part of her as the very air she breathed. Being without him was no longer an option. He was her everything.

As she settled into the driver's seat of her car, she reached for her phone, dialing a number she hadn't reached out to in quite some time.

"Pastor Felix, it's Ava," she said upon hearing the familiar voice on the other end. "I think you should contact the prayer circle. The coast guard has been called out to rescue two local teenagers who are missing out on the water. They're in need of all our prayers."

Chapter Thirteen

As soon as she reached the marina, Ava scanned the crowd, spotting familiar faces in the community.

Pastor Felix had made his way there in record time. Peggy Barnes, one of the members of the parent fundraiser group, was crossing her hands in front of her and seemed to be in the midst of prayer.

Dawson! She knew the name had sounded familiar earlier. Suddenly, it registered! He was Peggy's son. The one who'd been having problems fitting in ever since they'd moved to Buzzards Bay. The child who'd been closest to his father. And now he was out on the water and missing in unsafe conditions. Pretty soon it would be getting dark, which could make rescue efforts all the more difficult.

She quickly made her way over to the area where Peggy was frantically pacing back and forth.

"Peggy." She gently tapped her friend on the shoulder, unsure as to whether she should intrude at a moment like this. She turned around, her pretty face marred by worry lines. Her blue eyes were red rimmed from crying. She looked as if she were barely hanging on by a thread.

"Ava. I'm so glad you're here." Her voice broke as her entire body sagged. "We're waiting for word. The coast guard told us the Sea Hawk found Dawson and Chris alive, but they've alerted the medevac since they might be suffering from hypothermia."

Her lip trembled as tears pooled in her eyes. "What if he doesn't make it?"

"Don't think like that. He's alive, which is such a blessing. And he's been rescued." Ava reached for Peggy's hand and gripped it tightly. "I know all the members of that coast guard team and what they're capable of doing. He's in excellent hands."

Peggy let out a deep breath. "That's what Pastor Felix said. I've got to hold fast to my faith, especially in trying moments like this."

Ava gave her a smile of encouragement. She knew firsthand how difficult it was to stay strong in the face of adversity. "That's right, Peggy. I haven't always followed by that rule, but in the past few weeks I've realized that even when we're crying out in the darkness, He's always there. Listening. Pulling for us. Guiding us through the storms."

Tears pooled in her eyes as the words flowed out of her mouth. A sense of calm swept over her. Sometimes prayers were answered. And in this moment perhaps God was using her as an instrument to bring support to Peggy when she most needed it.

"Will you pray with me, Ava?" Peggy asked, her expression anxious, her eyes still filled with fear.

"Of course I will." She clasped Peggy's hand in hers and began praying, her voice strong and sure as they pleaded for their loved one's safe return.

As Sawyer maneuvered the Sea Hawk through Buzzards Bay Harbor, he spotted the twinkling lights of the dockside businesses in the distance. Bea's Fish and Chips. The Lobster Boat. Fresh Catch Fishing. A welcoming feeling hit him square in the chest. This was the place he called home. If he lived to be one hundred years old, he would never get sick of cruising into Buzzards Bay. The dock was lit up with torches and a group of people stood together, seemingly waiting for the rescue boat's arrival. From this distance he couldn't make out their faces, but he imagined the teens' parents were there, eager to make contact with their children. For the past twenty minutes he'd found himself thanking the Lord for His divine mercy.

By the time his team had located the teenagers, they'd been hanging on to their overturned sailboat and battling a raging surf. But for the grace of God, he truly believed they would have perished. There was no earthly reason they should have been able to endure the ocean's onslaught. As a man of faith he knew Dawson and Chris had been lifted up on God's shoulders. They'd been given a second chance at life. Once they had received medical treatment and had some food in their bellies, he planned to read them the riot act for their foolish behavior.

At the moment they were shell-shocked and hurting, most likely suffering from hypothermia. There would be plenty of time later for lectures about boat safety and responsibility. For now, they were all just grateful.

The sound of the medevac reached his ears above the whizzing motor of the surf rescue boat. He glanced up at the sky and saw it circling around, no doubt searching for a clear space to land near the docks. He glanced over at Bridget and Hank, who were sitting with the boys, both of whom were shivering despite being wrapped in blankets. His team was administering an oxygen protocol to stabilize their critical core temperature.

Experience had taught him that the first half hour during rescue was the most critical for hypothermia victims. As he guided the boat to the dock landing, he caught a glimpse of Ava standing on the edge of the crowd. Although his pulse spiked at the sight of her, he warned himself not to get too excited. He didn't dare hope she'd made her way down here for him. Those dreams had crashed and burned when she'd ordered him out of her house. Just knowing how she felt about him now caused a sharp pain to travel through him. The hurt was very raw, the wounds still gaping. He didn't even know if he could look her in the eye without shattering.

There was a woman standing next to her—auburn hair, a full, round face—he didn't need two guesses to know who belonged to her. Dawson was the spitting image of his mother. Ava had her arm around her shoulder and seemed to be comforting her. As they drew closer, he saw a look of joy sweep over the woman's face, followed by tears she was wiping away with a handkerchief. All the while Ava clutched her hand and never let go.

Disappointment seized him as reality began to sink in. She hadn't come for him. Clearly, she was friends with Dawson's mother, and it was for that reason she'd shown up at the harbor. He'd been foolish to think otherwise, especially since she'd made things between them crystal clear.

It was strange how even when he'd felt depleted of hope, he'd clung to that one, tiny kernel of it. That was love, he realized. It allowed you to hope beyond all reason, to dream of things that might never come to pass.

When he landed the boat at the pier the medical staff was lined up and ready to board the vessel. Raoul stepped off the boat to debrief Chris's and Dawson's families. The medevac would be taking the teens to the neighboring town of Hyannis, one of the few towns that had a full-fledged medical center. The teens were put on stretchers and taken off the boat. Bridget and Hank followed closely behind, wanting to see their mission through till the end. He would stick around on the boat to tie up any loose ends. The sight of the boys being reunited with their families was emotional. He prayed they would all realize how fortunate they were to be getting a second chance. Not all search-and-rescue missions had happy endings. His gaze locked with Ava's, and his throat convulsed as she began walking straight toward him, her stride full of purpose.

As she walked down the pier, her every step bringing her closer to him, his heart squeezed painfully in his chest. He felt an overwhelming need to sweep her up in his arms and hold her, to confess all the things he'd been holding back this whole time. He told himself to keep quiet. There was a good chance he might make a fool of himself if he opened up his mouth. Considering the way he felt, how his heart was beaten and bruised, there was no telling what he might say or do.

"Hi, Sawyer," she said in a breathless voice as she stepped on board the boat. "You should know that a lot of prayers were offered up on your behalf tonight."

He looked at her, slightly stunned that she was even speaking to him. The sight of her was awe-inspiring. It wasn't until this moment that he'd realized how much her absence had affected him. Just seeing her was slowly infusing life back into him. Her eyes were glistening, her hair glossy, cheeks reddened by the whipping wind. How he loved those beautiful hazel eyes. Need rose in him—a pure longing for this woman he loved—nearly knocking him off his feet. He steadied himself against the heady feeling, bracing himself for the possibility that she might lash out at him again.

Ava had already trampled over his heart and kicked him out of her life. What more was there to say? He just wasn't sure he could withstand any more heartache.

"Ava, what are you doing here?" Sawyer's tone wasn't exactly friendly. His eyes were dark and inscrutable, his tall frame stiff and unwelcoming. Her throat felt as dry as sawdust. He seemed so cold, not like the Sawyer she knew and loved. After the way she'd lashed out at him, she didn't blame him for being indifferent.

She was standing here with this big, gaping chasm between them and no idea how to cross it.

"I'm here for you. The same way you've always been there for me." Her voice rang out, full of certainty. Even though his body language made her want to turn tail and run, she held her ground. She was so tired of taking the path of least resistance. Some things were worth fighting for in this life. Sawyer was one of them.

"No need to worry," he responded in a gruff tone. "As you can see, I'm in one piece." He quickly turned his back on her, making it so she could no longer see his countenance. Not being able to read his expression gave her a panicky feeling in her belly. She needed to see his face, to watch his emotions as they moved across his face. His eyes always told her what he was thinking and feeling. More than anything, she needed to see herself reflected in his eyes, to know that they still had something worth fighting to save.

She reached out and grabbed him by the arm, feeling the corded muscles as she gently pulled it until he turned to look at her. "Sawyer. I need you to listen to me. I know I've hurt you. I know I laid some stuff at your feet that you didn't deserve. Blaming you for Billy's death—" Her words were swallowed up by shame. She couldn't even bring herself to finish her sentence. "I love you, Sawyer Trask."

Sawyer's head swung up and his chocolate-brown eyes skimmed over her face. He furrowed his brow, looking as if he were trying to make sense of what she'd just confessed. "You love me?" His voice came out raspy and rife with uncertainty.

"Always have. Always will," she answered in a voice full of emotion. "And I realize that I've made a huge mess of things. For so long I've been blaming myself… and God…for Billy's death. I couldn't seem to wrap my head around the fact that there really wasn't anyone to blame. Not myself. Not God. And certainly not you, Sawyer." She reached up and grazed her fingers across his face, feeling the stubble of a few days' growth prickling her skin as she worked her way across the landscape.

"People argue. They have disagreements. Sometimes we say things we don't mean. It's all a part of life and being human. I've had to face the fact that Billy made decisions that night. Just Billy. And he paid a terrible price for it. What happened when he took his boat out on the water was a sad, terrible thing. An accident. That's all it was. It's been a long journey to come to that realization, but I'm finally at peace with it."

Her nerves were shot and her pulse was racing. And Sawyer still hadn't said much at all in response to her declaration. Why hadn't he said anything? He was just standing there looking at her with a dazed expression on his face. For the life of her, she didn't know if that was a good thing or a bad thing.

"And you were right. I was scared of moving on, of taking a chance on loving someone else. For me, it's a terrifying concept to love someone so completely and then lose him. But I soon realized that being without you was the scariest thing of all. Because you're wonderful and honorable and you love my kids. And you have the biggest heart of anyone I've ever known. It doesn't get any better than that."

Sawyer was still staring at her, not saying a word. She was beginning to wonder if he'd had a change of heart. Her heart began to beat like thunder at the prospect. How badly had she messed up?

"I don't regret a single moment I spent with Billy. Without him I wouldn't have my two beautiful children. He helped shape me into the woman I am today. But I also believe that God has something wonderful in store for the two of us." She was twiddling her fingers now, filled with a nervous energy that she couldn't contain. If she only had her cross-stitch she'd be able to keep her fingers busy. Maybe she wouldn't be such a nervous wreck.

"Sawyer, please say something," she begged. She was practically handing him her heart on a silver platter. Hadn't he been moved by a single word she said? When she'd told him to go away, had she lost the opportunity to make a life with him? Had she scared him away for good?

"Can you just go back to the part about loving me?" he said. She watched his Adam's apple move as he swallowed. His eyes were brimming with emotion. "Because I don't think I'll ever get tired of hearing you say that."

"I love you," she said in a voice full of conviction. Sawyer took a step toward her and placed his arms around her waist. He lifted her up and spun her around, letting out a wild, exuberant cry in the process. When he placed her back down on solid ground, she had to hold on to his arm to steady herself from the dizzying sensations coursing through her. Or perhaps it was joy that was making her feel as if she were floating on air. Sawyer beamed down at her, his handsome face lit up with happiness.

"I love you, too, Ava. I always have," he whispered, his voice husky with emotion. She stood on her tiptoes and reached up toward him, hoping he would get the hint that she wanted to kiss him. Sawyer grinned at her and leaned down to meet her halfway, his lips moving over hers in a jubilant, powerful expression of everything they were feeling. His lips were warm and reassuring. Ava kissed him back with equal measure, wanting to show her undying devotion to the man she adored. As they broke apart from each other, Sawyer cupped her face in his hands, his touch full of tenderness. "And I always will," he vowed.

Epilogue

Ava lifted her face up to the sun and closed her eyes, enjoying the last blast of summer weather as the motorboat zigzagged across Buzzards Bay Harbor. The September wind was whipping through her hair as the salty smell of the ocean filled her nostrils. With Sawyer at the helm and the twins acting as his second-in-command, they were enjoying a leisurely outing at sea.

Over the past six weeks she'd been out on the water dozens of times with Sawyer. Although she'd been nervous at first, he'd put her at ease by taking it nice and easy on short trips across the bay. Seeing the joy on the children's faces was the best part of her conquering this particular fear. Being at one with nature and feeling a sense of absolute freedom as they glided across the water was a little slice of Heaven.

She felt the boat slowing down, and she opened her eyes to find them easing in as they arrived near the shore. They'd landed half a mile down the beach from her house and Sawyer's lighthouse. This hadn't been on the agenda, she realized with a frown. They should have landed at the marina.

"Look, Mama. We're at our beach," Dolly announced, looking very pleased with herself. Casey was looking back and forth between her and Sawyer, an expectant look etched on his face.

She cast her gaze toward him as suspicion swept through her. "Hey, Captain, what are we doing here?"

Sawyer just grinned and crossed his arms over his chest, trying to look innocent. He threw his hands up in the air. "Don't ask me."

Casey looked at Sawyer and asked, "Now?" Sawyer nodded and Casey dug into his duffel bag and pulled out a scroll of paper tied up with a gold ribbon. He walked over and handed it to his mother, his expression solemn as he said, "A lifetime's treasure awaits you."

"Is this what I think it is?" As she untied the ribbon and unfurled the scroll, she felt three pairs of eyes trained on her every move. She hadn't seen anything like this piece of parchment since she was a child. It was a treasure map, much like the ones Mr. P had made for her and Sawyer when they were kids. Joy bubbled up inside her. All of a sudden, she felt ten years old again.

The treasure map had a big X in the middle of it, with instructions laid out at the bottom. She looked up from the scroll. "Am I getting any help with this?"

Three heads shook, letting her know she was on her own. Treasure map in hand, she stepped off the boat, slipping off her shoes so she could navigate the sand better. Sawyer, Casey and Dolly followed behind her at a discreet distance. Meticulously, she went through the directions, making sure she didn't make any mistakes.

"Four steps west," she mumbled as she moved in that direction. One by one she followed the directions, occasionally reversing herself if she felt she made a mistake.

At last she ended up by the lifeguard chair. A bright green shovel was sticking out of the sand. A huge X had been made with shells, marking the area where she was supposed to dig. As soon as she began digging in the sand, the twins climbed the rungs of the lifeguard chair, perching themselves on the seat so they could watch her from on high. Sawyer stood a few feet away from her, watching her intently.

It didn't take very long until the shovel connected with a solid object. She used her hands to brush the sand away. A brass box lay nestled in the sand. She reached down and pulled it from its resting spot, flipping the lid open with childlike abandon. A small, velvet jewelry box lay inside and it was propped open to reveal a stunning ruby and diamond ring. Sitting next to it was a gold compass, eerily reminiscent of the one Sawyer had carried around with him as a child.

"Sawyer," she gasped. "What— Is this real?"

"It's real, baby. A ruby for devotion and a diamond for eternity."

Sawyer reached over and plucked the antique ring from its throne, holding it high in the air as he dropped to one knee in the sand. His eyes were full of love and admiration as he gazed at her.

"Ava, you're the most fearless woman I've ever known." He reached for her hand and brought it to his lips, pressing a kiss against her knuckles. "After what you've lost, you could have hidden yourself away for the rest of your life and licked your wounds. But you've embraced life and love. And I'm so thankful for that. You've faced your fears and dealt with them with courage and so much heart. I wanted Casey and Dolly to be here so they could bear witness to this moment. I love you, Ava. For most of my life you've been my best friend. I'd like to ask you to be my best friend, my compass, my love for the rest of our lives, till death us do part."

Ava nodded, tears coursing down her face as she held out her hand and answered, "Yes, Sawyer. A thousand times, yes."

How could there be any other answer but a jubilant yes? She wanted to love and be loved by Sawyer for the rest of their lives. The twins began clapping and cheering from up in the lifeguard chair. Sawyer reached out and placed the ring on her slender finger, rising from the sand as he did so. She tilted her head up to him, her eyes brimming with tears of joy. She felt the sun beaming down on her face, rays of healing light that mirrored what Sawyer had brought into her world. Joy. Companionship. Strength. Loyalty.

"You're my cornerstone. And my own personal hero. Nothing would make me prouder than to stand at the altar and pledge to you my undying loyalty and love. Forever."

Sawyer leaned down and captured her mouth with his in a triumphant celebration of two hearts joined in everlasting love. She wrapped her arms around his neck as she moved her lips against his, wanting the kiss to go on forever. Joy pulsed in the air around them. This was a perfect moment she would remember for all her days.

"I love you, I love you, I love you," she murmured against his lips, knowing that against all odds they'd found the love of a lifetime.

* * * * *

Dear Reader,

There are few places in the world I love more than Cape Cod. Lazy summer nights. The tangy scent of the ocean permeating the air. Warm sand in my toes. One of the best gifts my family ever gave my four siblings and me was the purchase of a summer house on the Cape. Now, my own children get to experience Cape Cod summers and the allure of Kalmus beach, Katie's ice cream, miniature golf and Main Street. Although Ava and Sawyer are the main characters, Cape Cod is the perfect backdrop for their love story. And I loved having a pair of twins in my book. Casey and Dolly are something else!

Forever Her Hero is a story of forgiveness, loss and second chances. Neither Ava nor Sawyer believe they are worthy enough to love one another due to their mutual guilt over Billy's death. In order to achieve their happily ever after, they first have to forgive themselves so they can embrace a love of a lifetime. In life, love and loss are oftentimes intertwined, and through God's grace and mercy we find a way to heal. As a writer I greatly enjoy the challenge of creating flawed characters who seek love, truth and understanding. And there's no ending better than a happily ever after. I am thrilled to be part of the Love Inspired team!

Thank you so much for reading *Forever Her Hero*. I truly hope you enjoyed this story as much as I enjoyed writing it. I love to hear from readers. I can be reached at scalhoune@gmail.com and my Author Belle Calhoune page on Facebook. I can also be found on my author website (www.bellecalhoune.com) and on Twitter (@BelleCalhoune).

Blessings,

Belle Calhoune

Questions for Discussion

1. Ava had a lot of anger toward Sawyer because he left Buzzards Bay for his mission in Africa. Why was she so deeply affected by his departure?

2. Sawyer comes back to Cape Cod determined to fulfill his obligation toward Casey and Dolly. What specific events influence him in this direction?

3. Ava has a lot of fears tied up with loss and survivor's guilt. How have her fears held her back and prevented her from moving forward?

4. Although Billy is deceased, he's a central figure in the story. What were Billy's strong points? His failings?

5. Sawyer has loved Ava for many years, but he buried his feelings out of respect for her marriage. Do you think he should have spoken up before Billy and Ava were married?

6. Everyone regards Sawyer as a hero due to his daring rescues. Why do you think he has such an issue with being called a hero? Is he a hero?

7. Uncle Troy is very threatened by the idea of Sawyer and Ava being together. Can you understand his feelings in the matter? Or was he being selfish?

8. Ava had to endure the loss of her parents and her husband's untimely death. Do you think God ever gives us more than we can handle?

9. Do you think Ava and Sawyer crossed any lines by falling in love? Why or why not?

10. At the wedding, Sawyer is very affected by Daniel's reading. "Many waters cannot quench love neither can the floods drown it." How did this passage relate to Sawyer and Ava?

11. Even though Ava is frightened by the ocean, she has great love for the sea and chooses to live near it. Have you ever feared and loved something at the same time?

12. What are the central themes of this story?

13. Sawyer waited two years to tell Ava about his argument with Billy. Is it understandable that he waited so long to tell her the truth? Why? Why not?

14. What are some of the challenges that occur when best friends have romantic feelings for one another?

15. Ultimately, what helped Ava get past the idea of responsibility for Billy's accident and accept the fact that she was in love with Sawyer?

REQUEST YOUR FREE BOOKS!

2 FREE INSPIRATIONAL NOVELS
PLUS 2
FREE
MYSTERY GIFTS

Love Inspired®

YES! Please send me 2 FREE Love Inspired® novels and my 2 FREE mystery gifts (gifts are worth about $10). After receiving them, if I don't wish to receive any more books, I can return the shipping statement marked "cancel." If I don't cancel, I will receive 6 brand-new novels every month and be billed just $4.74 per book in the U.S. or $5.24 per book in Canada. That's a saving of at least 21% off the cover price. It's quite a bargain! Shipping and handling is just 50¢ per book in the U.S. and 75¢ per book in Canada.* I understand that accepting the 2 free books and gifts places me under no obligation to buy anything. I can always return a shipment and cancel at any time. Even if I never buy another book, the two free books and gifts are mine to keep forever.

105/305 IDN F47Y

Name	(PLEASE PRINT)	
Address		Apt. #
City	State/Prov.	Zip/Postal Code

Signature (if under 18, a parent or guardian must sign)

Mail to the Harlequin® Reader Service:
IN U.S.A.: P.O. Box 1867, Buffalo, NY 14240-1867
IN CANADA: P.O. Box 609, Fort Erie, Ontario L2A 5X3

**Are you a subscriber to Love Inspired books
and want to receive the larger-print edition?
Call 1-800-873-8635 or visit www.ReaderService.com.**

* Terms and prices subject to change without notice. Prices do not include applicable taxes. Sales tax applicable in N.Y. Canadian residents will be charged applicable taxes. Offer not valid in Quebec. This offer is limited to one order per household. Not valid for current subscribers to Love Inspired books. All orders subject to credit approval. Credit or debit balances in a customer's account(s) may be offset by any other outstanding balance owed by or to the customer. Please allow 4 to 6 weeks for delivery. Offer available while quantities last.

Your Privacy—The Harlequin® Reader Service is committed to protecting your privacy. Our Privacy Policy is available online at www.ReaderService.com or upon request from the Harlequin Reader Service.

We make a portion of our mailing list available to reputable third parties that offer products we believe may interest you. If you prefer that we not exchange your name with third parties, or if you wish to clarify or modify your communication preferences, please visit us at www.ReaderService.com/consumerschoice or write to us at Harlequin Reader Service Preference Service, P.O. Box 9062, Buffalo, NY 14269. Include your complete name and address.

LI13R

Love Inspired

New family, new start

Harmony Cross is back in Dawson, Oklahoma, and determined to start over. She needs time and space—not complications. And definitely not Dylan Cooper, so it figures that she can't seem to stop bumping into him. But Dylan's been through a lot, too, and he's not the person he used to be. Now he's a single dad with two sweet and vulnerable children to take care of. Harmony never thought she'd see the day—not only is Dylan more kindhearted than she ever imagined, but she's falling for the last man she ever thought she'd love. If they can heal together, they just might build a new family…and the perfect harmony.

Single Dad Cowboy
by
Brenda Minton

Available June 2014 wherever
Love Inspired books and ebooks are sold.

Find us on Facebook at
www.Facebook.com/LoveInspiredBooks

LI87890